# The House
# on Old Mill Road

# THE HOUSE
# ON OLD MILL ROAD

*A Novel*

Victoria Frittitta

iUniverse, Inc.
New York Bloomington Shanghai

# The House on Old Mill Road

Copyright © 2008 by Victoria Frittitta

iUniverse books may be ordered through booksellers or by contacting:

iUniverse
1663 Liberty Drive
Bloomington, IN 47403
www.iuniverse.com
1-800-Authors (1-800-288-4677)

Because of the dynamic nature of the Internet, any Web addresses or links contained in this book may have changed since publication and may no longer be valid.

This is a work of fiction. All of the characters, names, incidents, organizations, and dialogue in this novel are either the products of the author's imagination or are used fictitiously.

ISBN: 978-0-595-48085-2 (pbk)
ISBN: 978-0-595-71864-1 (cloth)
ISBN: 978-0-595-60184-4 (ebk)

Printed in the United States of America

This book is dedicated to my children who provided me support and continuous encouragement toward completing this novel, a story that has haunted me for more than thirty years.

# PROLOGUE

▼

Summer is leaving,
Always weaving,
Through the seasons
To and fro.
Leaving places,
Sad'ning faces,
Summer's beauty
Has to go.

Written during a visitation by *The lady in her bedroom*
Donna Galassi at twelve years old.

The house was built entirely of locally milled wooden slats precisely nailed
into two-by-four lumber studs. The studs were secured to a foundation con-
structed from smooth round rocks roughly mortared with thick cement. Hidden
away underneath and inside the foundation, a basement was carved into the earth
at different depths. On the highest level, raised to accept the coldest and driest
air, was a root cellar. The dirt floor was littered with discarded hay bale cord and
remnants of rotted and dried crops. On a deeper level stood a massive wood and
coal burning heating unit that resembled a gothic crematorium that had been
used in the last century for some measure of comfort.

The four gabled peaks were adorned with gingerbread trim, scalloped moldings, and latticework. Double doors with diamond shaped leaded glass allowed a
graceful entrance into the front parlor. Once inside the exterior wood siding did
little to halt the cold blustery blasts of Adirondack air. On occasion, that frigid air

would whistle through the miniscule gaps of the outside slats. When the temperatures reached thirty below one could hear the rafters cracking under the weight of the frozen wooden shingled roof.

The house stood solidly in place for almost a century. It was born of love and determination. Eventually, the grief and anguish that played out within the confines of the lath covered plaster walls caused it to become haunted. Haunted by the pain and emotions of repetitive tragedies, the house ceased to provide its inhabitants with a warm comfortable experience. On the contrary, it occasionally conveyed an unnaturally uncomfortable feeling of despair and a sense of melancholy desperation. Little by little, an elusive sense of character was born between these crumbling walls, a character discerned telepathically more or less by the different people who occupied the premises.

With sporadic bursts of strength, the house began to take on a life of its own. Its hidden heart beat unceasingly, sequestered in the darkest corners of the upstairs hallway. Through some extrasensory vehicle, the house managed to orchestrate random events, allowing some inhabitants to feel an imagined sense of comfort and others to experience impalpable terror. This strength of character energized by events grew ever more powerful, ebbing and peaking at will. Sinister and terrifying, the house orchestrated a chain of circumstances that helped shape and change the lives of the innocent people who lived and loved within the confines of its impenetrable walls.

# THE BEGINNING

▼

Michael gently nudged Cammi with his elbow, and she rolled over mumbling something obscene. Her even breathing alerted him that she had fallen into a deep sleep again, so he dragged himself out of bed, walked to the crib, and adeptly gathered the tiny baby girl into his arms. He walked down the hall and peeked into Jenna's bedroom. He noticed she was undisturbed by her baby sister howling for her scheduled midnight bottle. *She must be used to the new baby.* He remembered the first few nights when Jenna would awaken at every tiny squeal from her new sister.

The four-ounce bottle was slowly heating in a pan of hot water on the stove when Cammi scuffled into the kitchen, her eyes squinting from the brightness of the light. Her dark curly hair was disheveled. It stood straight up in the back causing Michael to smile. Cammi leaned against Michael's muscular body and noticed their daughter Renee had peacefully dozed off while perched over his shoulder. Michael wore the infant's tiny body draped like a lion cub, her small arms dangling onto his back. Cammi yawned loudly, causing the baby to awaken and begin crying again.

"Now I understand why I married you. You're such a great husband."

Cammi folded her arms over her chest, shut her eyes, and relaxed against him. He gently rolled the nipple of the bottle into the baby's mouth, and Renee began sucking contentedly making tiny moaning sounds with each swallow.

"Go back to bed, honey. I have this shift covered," Michael said. "But, be sure the next one is yours. I have to meet the guys on the job at six-thirty. I'll make my sandwich and fill the thermos after I put Renee back in her crib."

He did not have to ask again. She thankfully kissed his shoulder and scuffled into the bedroom without another word.

Later, she awoke. Sunlight filtered through the broken venetian blind and struck her face. She reached over feeling for Michael's body on the other side of the bed and realized the mattress was empty. Most likely, he had already left for work. The baby was so content after her midnight bottle that she had slept through the early morning feeding time. Cammi could hear her older daughter Jenna happily singing nursery rhymes in her bed. She imagined her daughter with the covers pulled up over her head immersed in her own small world.

When Cammi drew the venetian blinds, she saw the makings of a glorious Long Island spring day. The birds were already scurrying from the treetops, swooping down onto the dewy grass, and gathering up whatever they could find to eat. She propped open the window and took a deep breath. As if on cue, little squealing sounds emanated from the direction of the crib, and then suddenly a strenuous struggle to work up to a high-pitched scream ensued. By the time Cammi could manage to pick up her daughter, Renee had succeeded in reaching a yelp, her legs stiff and her face beet red.

"My, my little girl, I'll get you some food after we change that poopy wet diaper of yours."

The apartment they had found in Bay Shore was in a centralized location making it easy for Michael to travel to work. They had scoured the newspaper listings for a long time before they found an affordable rental. At one time, this turn of the century gracious mansion had stood alone on the parcel of land that now contained a sprawling development that surrounded the property. Mature oak trees in the front yard, the tops intertwined, had overgrown the busy street. Years ago, the owner and his son had remodeled the home. They had divided it into four apartments, two on the upper and two on the lower floors. Cammi and Michael loved the spacious yard surrounded by an English rose garden that had fallen into disarray with weeds and wild blueberries everywhere, and that housed a swing set for the children.

After serving breakfast, Cammi dressed the girls. She thought Renee resembled a small doll wearing a pair of layered sweaters knitted by her grandmother. Her tiny arms stood stiffly out from her sides, and she was barely able to bring her clenched fist to her mouth. She was positioned inside her carriage, propped upon a pillow to give enough room for Jenna to sit inside the buggy beside her.

They followed a favorite path up some side streets to Main Street, now a seemingly decrepit part of town, the two story old buildings in dismal disrepair. Small, low-income shops occupied the antiquated spaces, very different from the new, high-end mall springing up on the six-lane highway located in the other direction. They first stopped at the shoemaker's shop to pick up the repaired leather hammer pouch Michael had torn on the job. Soon the baby fell asleep; her head flopped limply on her damp sweater where small spittle bubbles had formed and rolled down her chin. Cammi stopped to buy an ice cream cone for Jenna at the candy store on the corner of Main and Fifth streets.

Lulled by the movement of the carriage and the fresh air, Jenna curled into a fetal position inside the carriage and quickly fell asleep. Her mouth and chin was still sticky from the residue of the chocolate ice cream. The walk home was pleasant and quiet. Cool breezes fluttered Cammi's hair. She remembered how good it used to feel riding her old bike in Brooklyn when she was growing up. She wished her whole life would be as secure and sweet as it was this moment. She inhaled the fresh air deeply, thankful for the pleasant life she lived, and forever thankful for Michael and her family.

It was hard to remember life before Michael. When her family moved from Brooklyn, she was thirteen, and she felt terribly alone in this new strange place called Long Island. Being the new girl in town was also uncomfortable, and she tried to hide her shyness behind a façade of brashness. She struck up a new friendship with a girl in her ninth grade class named Lucille. Each time the teacher was distracted, the girls passed notes to one another during class, and they soon formed a close friendship.

One Wednesday afternoon during spring break, Lucille invited Cammi to come over and listen to records. The new sixties tunes were all the rage. Lucille's grandmother had baked chocolate chip cookies, and Cammi's mouth was full of cookies when she heard a car pull into the garage. Suddenly a young man appeared in the room. Cammi's jaw dropped. Lucille introduced the young man as her brother. He was the popular junior star running back for the high school football team. She tried hard not to stare at him, but he was gorgeous. He had long sideburns and thick black wavy hair. Michael winked at her with the most expressive green eyes she had ever seen as he carelessly shoved a whole cookie into his mouth. Her knees weakened when he smiled.

"I never saw him up close, just in the hallways going to class. He is really cute," Cammi said when she and Lucille were alone.

Lucille rolled her eyes.

"He's a jerk," she answered definitively. "All the girls think he's cute, but I have to live with him, and it sure ain't easy sometimes."

"Why?" Suddenly Cammi wanted to know everything about Michael.

"Just 'cause he's my brother. He even has the nerve to scare guys away and decide whom I can and cannot be seen with. He's a jerk, that's all!"

Cammi wanted to see Michael again. At every opportunity, she arranged to pass him in the hallway so she could wave at him from afar. She spent many afternoons at Lucille's house, but he was not always home. When the Fanelli family decided to throw a surprise party for Lucille's sixteenth birthday it was all Cammi could do to keep it a secret.

Cammi carefully chose her clothes for the party. She decided on a black sheath dress with a bright red scarf tied at the neck, and open flat shoes. Before the night was over Michael had noticed her quick wit, tiny turned up nose, and spectacular smile. They danced a slow dance toward the end of the party. Michael ran his hands up and down the small of her back, and he pulled her body tight up against his. He stepped back for a moment to look into the dark pools of her eyes. She swooned as she gazed into his green eyes.

"I think we need to set up a date to see each other again," he said.

Her heart skipped a beat. *Could it be this easy?*

"When?" She did not want to sound too eager, but could not help herself.

He took her hand and led her outside toward the garage decorated in a Hawaiian fashion for the party. They reached the front driveway and he turned and kissed her. Cammi melted into his arms. A month later he asked her to go steady. When he graduated, two years before her, they became engaged.

"Oh my God! Oh my God!" she yelled to Lucille, spinning around animatedly relating the details of her engagement.

"He asked me to marry him after I graduate!"

"That's cool," Lucille smiled.

"Since you have been seeing him, he has been a new guy, totally new, and such a better brother. I have to commend you Cammi; you bring out the best in Michael. Why, the first thing I noticed was he actually gave up on the school sluts. That was a big step for Michael, 'cause he loved those gum-cracking sluts hanging on his every word as though he were God himself. Lately, he has been hanging out more at home and playing his guitar. Wait until you hear, he even wrote a song especially for you."

Cammi began to hum that special tune as Jenna rolled over in the carriage. Her eyes opened for just a moment, but then she dozed off again.

As Cammi strolled closer to home, she noticed some of her neighbors had gathered in her backyard, taking advantage of the lovely weather. Marge was pushing little Tasha on the swing, Helen and Janet were sitting across from one another on the redwood picnic table while their children picked dandelion bouquets interspersed with other attractive weeds. As Cammi drew closer, she heard Janet giggling. "Do you suppose it will tell me if I'll get pregnant again tonight?"

"For that you'll have to talk to your husband," Helen smiled.

"Whatever are you guys up to?" Cammi asked, lowering her tone so as not to disturb her daughters from their nap.

She noticed they were laughing and talking about the Ouija board positioned between them on the picnic table. It was a game imagined by some to contact spirits from beyond the grave. Helen slid over to one side of the bench and motioned to Cammi.

"Got to try this thing, it's a riot. Tony and I played with it the last couple of nights and it is a lot of fun. There is different stuff it spells out for you. It actually guessed how many children we have and what I would cook for dinner, and of course, if we were going to have a frisky night at the Fricano residence."

Cammi stared at the Ouija board; she had never actually seen one but had read about the game in books pertaining to the supernatural. At one time, she had devoured books about Edgar Cayce, unseen forces and psychic experiences. She felt a creepy sense of fear and thought it best to restrain herself from trying out this newfangled neighborhood toy, so she stood back gawking at the game board.

"I don't really think I want to try it."

"Bachh, bachh chicken!" yelled Marge, who was still swinging Tasha.

"No, I just heard people talk about this type of game, and I think it might be a little dangerous," Cammi answered in a slightly shaky voice.

Helen laughed aloud. "Dangerous only if you have some deep dark secrets you don't want your husband to find out about. I don't really know how that thing moves anyhow, and sometimes the answers are pure gibberish. But, it does every so often answer questions you ask it."

Cammi glanced at her daughters who were still asleep inside the carriage. Feeling adventuresome, she slid onto the bench across from Janet.

"Just touch the tips of your fingers on the planchette." said Janet.

The small table began spinning in rapid movements around the board, picking up speed as it rounded the printed letters of the alphabet.

"Whoaaaaaaaaaa! Take a look at this thing move." Helen said, her eyes wide, an expression of disbelief on her face.

Marge grabbed Tasha from the swing, and ran to the picnic table to see what the commotion was all about. Frightened, Cammi removed her fingertips from the planchette and held her trembling hands clasped tightly on her lap.

"Go ahead. Try it again to see if the same thing happens." Helen said.

As she did, the game piece took on a life of its own and circled the printed alphabet in rapid motions, going around and around until it stopped and appeared to tremble, hovering over the letter *C*.

"I don't think this is for me," Cammi said. She glanced at Renee waking from her nap. She knew the baby would be cranky.

She reached into the carriage and picked up Renee, grateful for the opportunity to escape the Ouija board. She felt uncomfortable playing a game that was completely out of her mental control.

The next morning, Cammi heard the milk truck stop in front of her house. She took the steps two at a time to retrieve the bottles the milkman had left. She noticed the Ouija board propped up behind the Queen's Dairy wooden milk bin. She was reluctant to touch the board, but gingerly reached down to read the small note taped to the front of the game box.

*Whenever I play this game with Tony, it never reacted as it did for you. What with your babies waking from their nap while you were playing, I thought you would like to borrow it for a couple of days. Might want to play it with Michael, or maybe alone. Tony and I have had a ball with it, so have fun! Helen.*

Cammi could barely force herself to touch the damned game, but when she did, she felt a rush of relief. She grabbed the game board and deliberately carried it up the stairs and laid it on the kitchen table. Every time she glanced at the box, she reminded herself it was only a game inside. A game that played with your mind. An innocent piece of plastic and particleboard. *How dangerous can that possibly be?* After fixing breakfast for the girls, she secretively slid the Ouija board under the bed. The white eyelet bed skirt concealed it from view.

At two in the afternoon, while Renee was taking a nap and Jenna was playing with her friend down the street, Cammi had a little time to herself. She found herself unreasonably apprehensive, knowing she was too weak to resist the urge to play with *the damn game*. She slowly drew it out from under the bed and carried it into the kitchen, positioning it in front of her on the kitchen table. She gazed at it for a few moments trying to decide what frightened her so about the *damned thing*.

Diffused light from an overcast sky filtered through the orange curtains bathing the kitchen in a weird reddish color. Outside a misty rain fell silently on the roof. The ticking of the battery wall clock was the only sound that disturbed the silence. For the first time, she felt uneasy in her own home.

A knot formed in her stomach, and she felt herself begin to perspire as she lightly placed her fingertips on the planchette. The first touch sent it flying at horrific speed, broken only when she quickly withdrew her hands.

She sat for a quiet moment gaining her composure determined to overcome her fear. Thinking logically, she ran to get some paper and a pen so she could record the rapid movements of the planchette and make some sense of the letters it settled on. Three deep breaths quieted her pounding heart. She lightly placed her fingers on the planchette, anticipating the dizzying speed that would begin the session.

Feeling slightly more relaxed, the planchette appeared to mirror her emotion. It slowly began making large circular movements over the letters. At each pause, Cammi wrote down the letter it chose to stop on. After five minutes of recording each letter, she stopped in an attempt to decipher what she had written on her pad of paper.

*Iamhere malcolmhere iamhere malcolmhere*

"Who are you?" she asked aloud, dazed and disturbed at the same time. It surprised her that the gibberish had spelled out real words.

*Dunno*

"You have a name?"

*Malcolm*

"Who are you?"

She asked, quickly scribbling out each letter.

*Dunno*

"Where are you?"

*Dunno*

"What year is it?"

She paused in an attempt to gain her composure.

*eighteensixtythree*

"Did you die?"

*Dunno dunno war*

"What do you want with me?"

She was feeling confused and disoriented.

*Dunnoson*

"What?"

She carefully reread the words each letter had formed.

*Dunnoson*

"What are you saying? "

*Sonfindmyson*

She stopped to decipher her scribbling.

"Where is your son?"

*Dunno*

"How can I find him?"

She asked in a trembling voice.

*Dunnomaolcolmhere*

"How can I find him?"

She repeated, realizing the absurdity of the question.

*Youknow youknow dunno you know*

"How can I know?"

*Dunnoyou knowtheplace*

"What do I know?"

Cammi asked, cold chills creeping up and down her spine.

*Dunnotheplace youknowtheplace*

"But I don't know what you're talking about."

Her high-pitched voice echoed in the room, undeniably betraying the fact that she was on the edge of hysteria.

*Youknowtheplace youknowtheplace*

"What place?"

It was difficult for her to write quickly enough as the planchette raced from one letter to another.

*Dunno dunno dunno*

"How do I know?"

*You are me and I am you youaremeandiamyou*

The planchette paused for a moment as Cammi caught her breath.

*They want you back*

She was feverishly scribbling to keep pace with the letters.

*Theywantyouback theywantyouback theywantyouback*

Repeatedly the planchette passed over the letters, moved and stopped, moved and stopped, at break-neck speed. Cammi pulled her hands away to stop the motion. She stared at the written notes to decipher the last long series of letters. The hair prickled on her body when she realized what she had written. Frightened, she swept the game board off the table, and it flew across the room and smashed against the wall, the legs from the planchette broke into tiny pieces. A loud rumble that she thought was her heart beating was actually a burst of thunder that shook the very foundation of the house, and she involuntarily bolted from her chair.

Renee awoke and began screaming. Cammi ran to the crib, reached for her daughter, and held her tight to keep the infant's tiny body from trembling. Outside heavy gusts of rain pelted the roof making it difficult to hear her own heart pounding in her chest. She noticed the time and was astonished to realize that an hour had passed so quickly.

"It's okay baby, Mommy is here," she said, comforting Renee. "It's okay. It was only thunder, Mommy is here."

But it was not only the sound of the thunder that had caused Cammi to almost leap from her skin. She sensed something sinister had entered her life, and she had allowed it to happen out of curiosity. She allowed it to enter the sanctity of her home and eventually frighten her baby. She silently shook her head going over that last long jumble of words, *They want you back you are me, and I am you.*

What could that all possibly mean if anything?

Whatever it meant scared the shit out of her.

When the rainstorm calmed down, a neighbor dropped Jenna off at home. Once in the house, Jenna began rummaging through the many pieces of tiny pink girlie toys and baby dolls crammed into her toy box. Cammi went into the kitchen and swept up all the small plastic pieces from the game. She threw the objects into the box along with the game board. She slid the Ouija board back under the bed and made a mental note to return it to Helen first thing in the morning. It was something she did not want Michael to see, she was not prepared to speak to him about it right now. She decided she needed to make some sense of it in her own mind.

The truth was she was not ready to confess to him the sinister way she had whiled away the afternoon.

# MICHAEL

▼

The turkey sandwiches were a hit. Michael had stuffed himself eating the sandwiches and two heaping bowls of potato salad. He groaned a little as he lay back on the blanket with his knees drawn up and his head resting on his forearm.

"My God! This is heaven," he said, "A great lunch, and you."

He pulled Cammi down and playfully pinned her arms to her sides. Kissing her gently, he stroked her long black curls.

"So, does it still feel good being Mrs. Fanelli?"

"I cannot believe it's already our fifth anniversary. It feels like fifteen."

She giggled.

He playfully nuzzled at her neck.

"It was nice to have your mother take the kids so we could get a weekend alone. It would not have been the same with them running around here demanding attention."

"Oh yeah, I could see them now with us splashing around in the water trying to maneuver that canoe we tipped over this afternoon."

They both laughed at the recollection of the sight of their cooler as it slowly meandered downstream while they struggled to roll the canoe upright. They swam together towing the canoe to within ten feet of the shoreline and climbed back in. They paddled quickly toward the cooler still bobbing on the surface. After they retrieved it, Cammi was horrified to realize alligators lived along the banks of the waterway.

Michael just smirked when he informed her of that.

They had flown to Florida. There, Cammi's parents owned a condominium they used only three months every winter. Each morning Michael and Cammi relaxed by the pool, and in the afternoons they made the rounds of the Shell Factory and the Fort Myers Beach Pier.

Now they lay together in their wet clothes on the muddy banks of the river. Feeling amorous, Cammi ran her hands lightly over her husband's smooth, hard muscles all the way down his arm to his fingers.

"Ouch!" he yelped.

"Is that thumb still hurting?"

"Hurting? It's still killing me."

He held up his thumb to display the huge blood blister that had formed after he had smacked it with a hammer. The thumb was still a sickening purple and yellow color, even though it had happened more than a week ago.

"My true initiation into the crackpot carpenters union. The guys always kidded me that I had a perfect record until that day. I mean I was a legend in my own time."

They laughed.

"But, they sure gave me a great initiation party. Now I am not a virgin carpenter anymore. They accused me of hammering like a pussy before that, now they know I'm one of the veterans. When I lose the nail, it will be another party time. Small things amuse small minds."

"You would not have smashed that thumb so badly if you didn't work out so hard to bench press two fifty." She grinned at him and his face lit up.

He pulled her down so she could cuddle in his arms. He kissed the side of her head, and together they gazed up at the blue sky that peeked through the tops of the trees.

"Ouch … again!" Michael cried out.

She had smacked a huge mosquito that had landed on his shoulder.

"Man, you know I got too much sun yesterday."

"We are sounding like a couple ready for the senior afternoon dinner special," she said.

They laughed again, feeling giddy.

"We needed this time alone together; I mean we didn't even have time for a honeymoon after we got married," Michael said.

"Well, remember I was pregnant with Jenna then. We needed every bit of money just to get an apartment."

"Your mother should have let me marry you when we had planned it and not have to wait for the big wedding thing," Michael said.

"Oh, come on, that was really nice."

"Yeah, but we had to wait so damn long. You knew I fell in love with you the first day I laid eyes on you, cookie crumbs and all."

"Will you stop whining," she said.

"You know, this morning I saw something on the bulletin board about an amateur palm reader having a demonstration at poolside tomorrow afternoon at the Spa Club."

"Do you mean like palm trees? Otherwise, if you mean what I think, honey, don't drag me to see that crap."

"What? Is it not manly to believe in a palm reader?" she teased.

"No, it's not that, it just doesn't make any sense to me at all. Hocus pocus stuff is for small minds."

"Well, thank you very much," she said, feigning anger.

"You can go for fun, honey, but don't go falling off a cliff believing in that crap."

She pretended to be hurt. "And all along I thought you knew I was a witch."

"I realized that lots of times, baby, lots of times."

She smacked him again.

"Hope your sunburn hurts worse now."

"No, seriously, honey. Do you believe in that crap?"

"Well, I used to read a lot of books about it, and I have had some simple experiences like knowing who is calling before I answer the phone or knowing what someone is thinking. But it doesn't happen very often, just once in a while."

She cocked her head to the side, thinking.

"Actually, I believe it was four times in my life. And one time I had a dream the neighbor's dog died, and the next day it was her husband that bit the dust."

"Whooooo," he said, waving his fingers in the air, "You are really scary, lady. You mean to tell me you dream the dog dies and it's the husband who dies. Not saying much for the masculine gender, lady. I thought you had me on a pedestal. Don't let me hear you say stuff like *sit* or *give me your paw*."

She shook her head, "Screw you, I am trying to be serious."

"I believe you. Really!"

They were already in such a giggling mood that Cammi did not approach him with the story of her Ouija board experience from a couple of years ago. *Maybe it's best left unsaid after this much time.* She decided not to go to the planned demonstration in the morning.

# Young Benjamin Robert Treadwell, Jr.

▼

Keep hammering, keep making a racket and maybe she'll go away.

He kept at it incessantly, the pounding of a hammer hitting nails resonated throughout the valley. The noise bounced back as a high-pitched echo from the surrounding mountains. It was *his* tree fort, *his* cry for independence, *his* special place where his father allowed him to build to his heart's content. He was allowed permission to split wood and use whichever tools were considered necessary, short of the heavy machinery only the stronger men were able to use.

Usually, he mischievously, on a mission to annoy the heck out of his grandmother, just made a whole lot of noise. It was a futile attempt to tune her out.

If I keep hammering, she'll think I don't hear her calling me inside.

She had prepared lunch for the boy, warm soup, and fresh baked bread. Two apple pies, a gift from the fruit laden tree—sat on the pantry shelf. The glorious scent of cinnamon and apples filled every room in the house. During cool weather, the wood burning stove was stoked high, and a massive kettle of water simmered on the rear burner that provided moisture and a quick cup of Chinese tea. Now that fall had taken hold, the air was brisk, sometimes overcast, with a frigid drizzle of rain. A vigorous snow would come soon. She knew this from years of experience living here in these mountains. This morning the drizzle had tapered off and the sun partially peeked out from behind the clouds, creating a shiny tapestry of leaves that now littered the ground. The damp, bright red and gold leaves glistened from the earlier rain so that one could not hear the leaves crunching under foot.

Suddenly she was there. She grabbed Benny by the back of his collar and hauled him into the house, hammer still clutched in his hand. He dug his heels into the wet earth in a feeble attempt to halt her progress. He was always surprised at how much strength she could exert from those bent, misshapen fingers.

In a stern voice with a slight hint of British, she took full command of the situation.

"It is lunchtime, young Ben. Food is hot and prepared. You pretend never to hear me over that racket you make with your hammer. Get inside young man, and wash the filth off those hands."

Benny reluctantly placed his hammer beside the washbasin.

"Yes, ma'am," he answered, finally subdued and hoping to avoid one of her notorious swats on the seat of his pants.

God she is tough, he thought. He had heard the stories about just how tough his grandma really was since he was very little, and he reckoned every story was true.

Grandma Mildred gracefully maneuvered around her comfortable kitchen, making even the most difficult chore appear effortless. The mahogany pedestal table had been set for three, Benny's little sister Catherine was already seated and, was in the process of slurping soup from her small spoon. His grandma set a steaming bowl of delectable chicken soup at Benny's place. Only then did he feel the emptiness in his stomach, and realized he was hungry.

He recalled the time she had ceremoniously, and in low solemn tones, spoken to him about the grandfather he never knew. That was the only time Benny noticed her eyes become soft and gentle, as she mournfully remembered and longed for the days of her youth.

Grandfather Malcolm had been a handsome young man who sat tall and proud. He and Grandma Mildred met when they were young children, immigrants who accompanied their parents on a long journey across the sea. After disembarking, fifteen families had set off by wagon route overland to St. Charles, Missouri, after hearing a rumor that there was work available for boat builders in that part of the country. Twelve of the fifteen families arrived intact, and they settled in a small town nestled in close proximity to the river.

On a bright and sunny day along the bustling riverfront, the two children had run into each other after being apart for about one year. Mildred was a beauty in the days of her youth. A soft spoken, tiny corseted wisp of a woman, whose puffy cotton sleeves concealed the muscles she had developed through hard labor. The couple had secretly hoped to meet again; Mildred made several mentions of this in the small diary she kept hidden inside the straw of her mattress. The timing of their reunion was perfect, and they were hastily married in 1861.

The first months of their marriage were passionate and exciting, and Mildred envisioned fervent wishes and dreams for their promising future together. On the day she discovered she was pregnant, she overheard heated talk from the men on the streets, talk of war that caused commotion and unrest. Little by little, young men began to enlist, to protect the honorable cause of whichever side they chose. Mildred tried to keep her young husband home by pleading with him not to join the army, but Malcolm was persuaded to enlist by the furor and excitement that defined the early war years. He was positive that the uprising would last only a few months and determined he would soon be home to attend the birth of his child. He would then nestle in Mildred's comforting arms forever.

They traveled together to St. Louis to stock enough staples and supplies to keep Mildred fed for approximately six months. They bought flour, sugar, a dozen chickens to produce fresh eggs, eighteen young turkeys, and two young pigs. Malcolm slaughtered a deer and set it to cure. He split enough wood to last until spring. As he set out to join his regiment, he promised fervently a hundred times, no, a thousand times that he would return to her. They both reasoned he was too young to die. Sadly, her husband never returned home. Their last moments together were forever burned into Mildred's memory.

Malcolm's regiment had been camped at Meridian Hill, within sight of the White House. They received orders to join the Army of the Potomac, and then marched across Long Bridge into Virginia to set up camp a few miles southwest of Alexandria. He successfully carried out a number of reconnaissance missions. However, near the shore of the Rappahannock River, his horse slipped on some rocks and the cavalryman was thrown to the ground. His horse landed on top of him. Malcolm never regained consciousness. He died two days later at a field hospital. A minié ball had not killed poor Malcolm, but fate decided he would never go home to Missouri again. Mildred bore him a son a few months after his death.

The following year, with the provisions gone and the cords of wood burned into ashes, Mildred and her young son Benjamin bravely ventured into St. Louis. There she met up with a handsome young trapper from Canada. He promised her the moon. What she got was a hard trip over land by wagon, and a long over-water trip by ferry to the great Adirondack Mountains.

It was a *"howling wilderness"*[1] during those years. A wild land built of prime pine and spruce and sphagnum moss. Embryonic water kettles dotted the landscape creating a rain place that millions of years before had been shaped by powerful forces of nature.

At the very least, the trapper had provided Mildred and her son with a destination. It was not one she would have chosen, but nonetheless, another starting point in her short, tragic life. There were long hours of drudgery work, but Mildred struggled to stay alive. Before the trapper moved north into Canada, in a protective spirit, he provided her with a small shanty shelter with dirt floors and greased paper windows—pitiful protection from the violent winter weather ahead.

In order to eke out a pitiful living, Mildred took in wash from the trappers and guides when they came into town. The men would instinctively find their way into this small village searching for a place to clean their clothes. Important to them was a much needed warm bath and bed for the night. Crossing the brook at the foot of the hill to the small shanty where she lived and worked, she would welcome each paying guest with a meager meal and a place on the dirt floor to sleep. These were difficult years, and on some days, Mildred wondered if she and the boy would survive this dark wilderness.

The meals Mildred could provide mostly consisted of beans and potatoes that she had bartered for. On occasion, the trappers would pay for their washed clothes and services with a piece of venison or a wild turkey or a grouse. Before long, wild muskrat skins, beaver pelts, and otter fur covered the floors of her shanty providing crude beds on the earthen floor. In the evening, when Mildred put Benjamin down to sleep, she would sit up late into the night and listen to the howl of the wolves outside her cabin. On occasion, long drawn-out tales from men, unaccustomed to having anyone around to listen would entertain her.

In early spring, Mildred tapped nearby maple trees and boiled down the sap to make maple syrup, a prized commodity for her customers. She also sold small amounts of potash, the remnants of the sap, to make soap for her meager enterprise. Through hard labor and intense persistence, Mildred and her son began to thrive.

---

1. "Generally speaking, a howling wilderness does not howl; it is the imagination of the traveler that does the howling," Thoreau in *The Maine Woods*.

She insisted the youngster attend school. He was not the brightest student, but he quickly grasped from his mother the qualities of perseverance, determination, and patience required to achieve success.

When he was twelve years old, he was an apprentice carpenter and laborer who helped to build Adirondack cabins for the wealthy tourists who dared venture into the wilderness. By the time Benjamin Treadwell was fourteen, he had become an experienced lumberman during the summer. During the winter months, he was employed at the St. Regis Hotel. His education terminated when his mother's rheumatoid arthritis worsened. It prevented her from doing continuous strenuous work with her hands. Now the tables were turned. Benjamin had to provide for his aging mother.

He was twenty when he married Elizabeth Mary Morgan. He envisioned prosperity in the business of building, so he educated himself at night by the light of a kerosene lamp. He built a small mill outside of town and was able to advance his knowledge in the business. He enrolled in a correspondence course in architecture and perfected plans for large camps on the lakes, much desired by the wealthy class. His vision extended beyond school teachings, and he continued to develop, utilizing his inborn tenacity and admiration of physical labor. She had taught him very early in life how to survive the physical elements and the mental desires.

For no particular reason, Benjamin and Elizabeth did not have children right away. Finally, one rainy day in May of 1898, Benjamin Robert Treadwell Junior was born. Young Benny was a healthy, strapping baby. When he could barely crawl, he picked up anything that remotely resembled a hammer and pounded the wall, the floors, and the steps. He was almost four when he began entertaining himself with hammering nails into every piece of wood he could find. One time his father set a chalk line and Benny would follow nails straight across head to head.

Daughter Catherine was born one and a half years later, but obviously, his father favored Benny. On days off from school, young Benny was the one chosen to accompany his father across the lake to check on the progress of each new construction site. Benjamin explained to his son all the newest trends that were rapidly becoming fashionable as though the child was his peer. Young Benny loved the feel of wood in his soft small hands, molding it with imaginative creativity. His father was his mentor and sidekick for as long as he could remember. Benny loved the smell of newly sawed sawdust and he quickly developed a keen eye for architecture.

Grandma Mildred was always in charge of lovingly caring for the family. Her arthritic fingers did not hinder her from baking pies and breads of all kinds. Her special joy was in the art of making jelly and fancy Christmas cakes with green and red icing. What came in short supply was her patience for children. She believed they needed stricter supervision and tighter rules in hopes they would learn to behave more obediently toward her.

Benny connived if he was in a tight spot with Grandma, his father would bail him out. One time Grandma had caught him playing with matches, and he took a pounding from a large wooden spoon on his rump. Afterwards, it took his father several hours to coax Grandma to release the boy from the confines of his room. Benny eventually learned to respect what his grandmother taught him, but he had moments of stubborn independence that he was sure caused her extreme anguish.

Sadly, soon after Benny turned twelve, his grandmother died unexpectedly. It was then he experienced raw feelings of upheaval and loss, because she had literally raised him since birth. His father took it hard, too. He locked himself in his office, carrying with him several bottles of Irish whiskey, and he stayed secluded for five days.

Finally, one day he emerged, his face unshaven and his clothes disheveled. It was the first time his father spoke emotionally to his family of the love he felt for his mother. This revealed to Benny a side of his father that he had never known. His father explained how he had appreciated the unwavering care and guidance his mother had provided him his entire life. His detailed revelations described the years of hard labor and the energy expelled to miraculously enable survival.

Meanwhile, Benny's mother, Elizabeth Mary, had managed the mill office since its inception. She exerted firm control of her life as a full-time working woman. The townsfolk viewed her as an enigma, and although she was socially accepted, she never quite fit in with the locals. She willingly helped her husband study at night for his correspondence classes, and tested him on his study material. Thus, it increased her knowledge in the trade. Consequently, when she became interested in the inner workings of the mill, she brought with her full knowledge of the building trade.

When the revolutionary idea of setting skylights into roofs was developed, she convinced her husband to install two, in different parts of their house as a test project. Prospective customers who wanted to see how they were installed would stop by to inspect the skylights. Meanwhile, the family enjoyed the newest innovative alterations to their home.

At the main office, she ordered stock, kept the ledgers, and handled correspondence. No one realized that when she and Benjamin were alone at night, she had become the driving force behind the man. She gathered unprecedented ideas from her mill customers. Architecturally, she changed previously accepted plans to incorporate another room. She thought nothing of resituating a fireplace or creating innovative use of cabinetry in the pantry area.

Elizabeth and Benjamin had purchased land on the Old Mill Road soon after Benny was conceived. Consequently, all young Benny ever knew was that house. He was born in it, and believed he would most likely die in it.

In the early phases of construction, the house was an eight-room structure, but, as jobs became more profitable and the family amassed wealth, they added onto the home. It eventually stood as a shining monument to the dignity and financial fortune of the Treadwell family.

A British gardener was hired to add elegant flower gardens to the front grounds and to maintain the lush green lawn on the thirty-acre parcel. The house, built around a center courtyard, eventually increased to number fourteen rooms. The courtyard rooms received significant light from windows built into both sidewalls. On one end of the lower level guest quarters, a porch was situated adjacent to the children's playroom. The breakfast room had access from the kitchen through a sparkling glass and ornate carved oak breakfront, situated as a divider to the room. A magnificent gleaming wood burning stove dominated the red Mexican tiled kitchen with a multipurpose service pantry located close by the kitchen entrance from the living room. Graceful carved wooden scrollwork decorated the living room window alcove, brightened on gloomy winter days by the overhead skylight. The carved fireplace mantel curved gracefully around side bookshelves enclosed with leaded glass, diamond pane doors. Upstairs were five bedrooms, all special and unique, with custom-built closets and storage space adorned with thick decorative moldings and trim.

It was apparent to the family that Benny suffered greatly after the loss of his grandmother. All those years of stubborn disobedience caused him to feel pangs of guilt because of the way he treated her while he was growing up. So to help in his emotional adjustment, his father entrusted him with a small job. It was to complete the porch enclosure, which had begun under Grandma's watchful eye. While still alive, she had meticulously planned for the porch to be an area where she could sit comfortably and bask in the summer sun. She said she needed to bake some warmth into her aching bones. Her rocking chair, positioned in a place of honor, enabled her to view the entire front yard.

Benny was sorry she did not live long enough to take advantage of the remodeling changes of the porch area. He knew she would have been deliriously happy to garden and transplant her favorite potted geraniums, all the while escaping the wrath of the annoying black fly season. He arranged with his mother to mill the wood trim he needed for the job. Precision milled windows had been installed half-way around the house during the past year, but the job was never completed.

As a special surprise for his father, Benny hand carved one decorative pillar support for the porch that he displayed at the entrance and mounted conspicuously in front of the double entrance doors. Beautifully scrolled, Benny reverently sanded smooth the embossed carvings. The wood felt pliable, almost flesh-like in his hands. Creating this final change was a thrill for the boy, and he could not decide if he created it more out of his love for his grandmother or for his father. Benny felt an immense sense of pride when he caught the gleam in his father's eye, as his father watched him set the decorative pillar in place.

With his experiences speeding up his maturity, Benny's education rapidly exceeded that of his father's. Benny was an accomplished student attending a small school down the road. Mrs. Goodspeed was his favorite teacher. He was a boy in constant motion while growing up, horsing around, attending to studies, and completing daily chores.

During this frantically busy period, a two-story building was erected about fifty feet behind the Treadwell's house. Floor plans designated the second story of this structure to house in bunk-room style, the seasonal help, laborers who worked for the Treadwell enterprise. The lower level provided ample storage for stock items like windows, doors, trim, lathe, cement mixers, roof shingles—everything down to barrels of tenpenny nails.

The upper quarters quickly became a weekend social club for the workers. Late on Friday and Saturdays nights, when the house was quiet and everyone was asleep, Benny would sneak out of his bedroom to join the labor crew. There he was entertained with off-color jokes and overblown tales of each individual's sexual prowess. There was bragging and kidding about that very first sexual encounter, the first naked breast ever touched, and stories of first genuine true loves.

Considered one of the guys, Benny was offered a plug of tobacco or locally distilled whiskey. The crew provided him tawdry primer lessons about life and true love before puberty indoctrinated him naturally. But the most outstanding draw to the group was that they taught him to play poker. Oftentimes, Benny would sit in on games with the stakes higher than a week's salary. When he lost, the men really did not expect him to reimburse them, but they kept a chalkboard tally of his debts. Soon his credits began to accumulate.

# Marie and Ron

▼

Cammi dropped Jenna off at kindergarten and then walked over to Marie's house on Bay Shore Road to join her for a cup of coffee. Those ten extra pounds she gained after giving birth to Jenna had still not melted away, and since she enjoyed walking, she considered this her free treadmill exercise. She smiled recalling the unusual circumstances that had connected her to her friend.

Renee and Jenna had been playing in the sand pile in the outside yard by the apartment when suddenly Cammi heard Renee crying.

"What happened, baby?" Cammi asked, picking up her daughter who now weighed about thirty pounds.

"He punched me," she said, pointing to a little boy running toward a house.

"Oh my God!" Cammi said, as Renee retched and then vomited.

Cammi marched herself and both girls to the house the little boy had entered. After several loud knocks on the door a woman responded and invited Cammi inside. The woman, slightly built, had her long hair tied in a ponytail that reached her waist. She smiled pleasantly at Jenna and Renee and offered her hand. The girls, slightly embarrassed, hung back behind their mother.

"Your son punched my daughter in the stomach. She felt confused and disoriented." Cammi said.

In another room, the boy was crying hysterically.

"Oh honey, I'm sorry," Marie said, speaking directly to the girls.

"I don't think he really meant it."

"What are you saying … he didn't mean to do it?" Cammi was losing her cool. Michael chided her all the time that her temper was short when it came to her children.

"Jimmy," Marie called. The small boy came out of a bathroom with a wet towel wrapped around his arm, tears streaming down his face. Marie removed the towel and held his arm out for Cammi to see. Small tooth marks were visible on his forearm, and he was bleeding.

Shocked, Cammi turned to Renee and asked, "Did you do that?"

"Yes."

"And then he punched you in the stomach to make you let go?"

"Yes."

"Wait for me one short moment," Cammi said to Marie. She stepped outside and reprimanded Renee.

When Cammi came back into the house, Marie had a cup of steaming coffee waiting for her on the counter.

"Please, sit down," Marie offered. "That's why I never get too involved in situations regarding the kids. Circumstances are never what they seem. You always have to hear the other side of the story."

Cammi felt her cheeks warm, and she apologized. Both women sat the whole morning talking as the children played together in the next room, acting as though nothing had happened. It was instant friendship.

Marie's husband Ron was a police officer, brash and outspoken, and he held firm control over Marie and their two sons. But he and Michael hit it off famously, and both couples shared many a Saturday night at one another's houses playing cards while Jenna and Renee played with Jimmy and Anthony.

"Throw the friggin' queen," Cammi pleaded with Ron while playing cards one night, but he held tight and ran the deck causing everyone to lose the game.

He smirked, "I have smarts," he said, "and balls, and that's a winning combination."Cammi shoved her cards across the table and smiled.

"Balls, maybe, but I am not so sure about the smarts."

"You've got to be smart to be a cop."

Cammi did a double take in his direction.

"Or suicidal," she answered.

He scooted backward in his chair, his legs outstretched, his arms folded over his protruding belly.

He smirked again.

"You're just sore that you didn't have the hand I had to run the table."

Cammi just smiled.

It had become a pleasant weekly event teasing the winner. Their personalities blossomed and melded together and formed an even stronger friendship bond.

That night driving home with Michael, Cammi rehashed the events from the evening.

"Ron is so pushy."

"You're the pushy broad," he answered.

"I am not!"

"Well, you do like being in control. Isn't that right, honey?"

"Right."

"Well …, that makes you a pushy broad."

"I like the word independent lots better," she said.

"Semantics, only semantics."

"What? Independent means pushy broad?"

He reached across the seat and put his arm around her shoulder.

"Pushy, independent broad, get over here, I love you."

She smiled, fully admitting she was that and more.

# The Journey

▼

Reminiscing years later, Cammi could not recall the precise moment when the planets moved in conjunction that defined her family's long journey into the mountains. Unexpected events were somehow predestined to lead the family to its final climax. There were outside pressures and forces that drew the Fanelli family to that one point in time, that one particular place on the planet that would alter their lives forever.

The next few years found the couple immersed in a humdrum existence that involved the daily chores of raising a family. Michael had become lead carpenter, but the money he managed to make was never enough. He was able to get some side jobs whenever he could.

Cammi worked part time in the library in the mornings to earn extra money for the children. She and Michael had hoped that by this time, they could have afforded to purchase a home, but the dream seemed out of reach just yet.

An unexpected announcement quickly changed their daily schedule of events.

The downstairs entrance door slammed, Michael yelled for Cammi as he noisily took the steps two at a time. He burst into the apartment.

"What the hell?" Cammi asked.

"Honey," his face was red, and planted on it was the biggest grin she could ever recall. He waved a small piece of paper in his hand.

"Look at this, baby!"

Cammi blinked at the folded paper he shoved at her, grabbed it, and tore it open.

"What is going on?" she said, trying to concentrate on what she was reading.

"Read it, baby, read it."

She sat down slowly, shaking her head in disbelief.

"Fifteen thousand big ones in the New York State Lottery!" he yelled at the top of his lungs.

She screamed in happiness, and tears ran down her cheeks.

When the children came into the front hallway, the couple was dancing, and although the children did not quite comprehend the situation, they knew something really special had happened. So, they started dancing with their parents. Before long, neighbors stopped by and Michael excitedly told them about their unbelievable windfall.

"It's ours," he said when he and Cammi were alone. "And tomorrow we are going to talk vacation, do you hear me, baby? We are going on a vacation, anywhere you choose. But, that's after I put a down payment on a family station wagon. Yahoo!"

He flopped into the nearest chair, exhausted from all the excitement, and fanned his face with the paperwork. He stared at the winning ticket as though etching the numbers in his memory. Cammi fell into his arms and the girls piled into their laps.

The next afternoon, Cammi heard a car horn beeping outside. She poked her head out the window and saw a station wagon parked in front of the house. She and the girls raced down the stairs and screamed with joy when Michael emerged from the new Ford Fairlane Squire wagon. It was black on top with natural wood trim, a 1967 model vehicle. He walked around to the passenger side and opened the door for Cammi. She proudly slid into the front seat.

"I love it!" she said, running her hands over the plush red leather seats, while checking out all the room in the rear of the car.

"Get the kids in the back and I'll take you for a ride." Michael was dying to drive around and show off his new car.

"Check out the radio, baby." Michael turned up the sound to a deafening level. The girls held their ears. The perfectly tuned speakers belted out "Sunshine of Your Love," quickly followed by "Hey Jude."

"Sweet!" Michael said with a smile of pure contentment.

Once they were on the highway, he asked Cammi, "Have you thought about where you want to go? This sweet little wagon will take us anywhere in pure comfort."

"I'd like to go upstate again," she said. "Remember how nice it was when we drove through there a couple years ago? Well, maybe this time let's continue driving north of Albany. I saw advertised in the newspaper a place in the Adirondack Mountains called Santa's Workshop up by Whiteface Mountain, and I think it would be a lot of fun for everyone. Maybe stop off in Saratoga Springs or Glens Falls, or how about continuing north on the Northway to Montreal? What do you think?"

"I think north it is," Michael agreed.

"Adirondack's look out. Here come the Fanellis!"

# Benny Treadwell
# The Arrival

▼

"Your aunt Geraldine is coming to live with us. You've never met her because she always lived in Rochester, and for whatever reasons, she never made it up here to visit. Your mother hasn't seen much of her either, since before we were married. They write occasionally, and keep in touch, as sisters do, but I'm not familiar with her."

Benny and Catherine were listening intently to their father and knowing that what he was saying was going to be an adjustment to their daily household life. Benny studied his father who appeared somewhat preoccupied as of late. Today, his father was animated, chewing on the ever-present cigar butt, adeptly rolling it around in his mouth as he spoke. Brown stained spittle rolled slowly down to his chin. He removed his hands where they rested inside the bib top jeans and wiped away the spittle with his checkered shirtsleeve. He removed his hat to scratch at the small bald area that had begun to appear on the top of his head.

"She has a boy …, I believe Floyd is his name. I've heard he is a wimpy sort of effeminate kid. Never was exposed to wild country life like we have here. They're city people, but since the husband of Geraldine passed, they've fallen on hard times. Your mother thinks it will be a fine and accommodating arrangement for all of us. Anyway, Geraldine is supposed to be an experienced cook. Thank the good Lord for some small positives."

He stuffed the limp felt hat back on his head. He looked a little silly because the hat had shrunk and was too small for his head.

"How old is Floyd?" Benny and Catherine asked in unison.

"Oh, from what your mother tells me … eight or nine. At least he is no longer a sniffling young child who cries a fit ten times a day."

Benny sulked while kicking at some stones and did not reply.

"You Benny, I expect you to oversee the boy, until he gets adjusted to life here. I don't want him getting into mischief or getting hurt, hear?"

"Yes, Pa." There was no enthusiasm in his tone.

"I think it would be a good arrangement to maybe work him into managing some chores in the barn. You can show him what to do."

"But, Joe works the barn, always has since his Pa came here to live two years ago."

"Joe works the barn and does a fine job of it, but he can always use some help caring for the team. There is leather to be conditioned, hay to be put up, and stalls to keep clean. Besides, it takes some time to get used to being around them draft horses the size they are, and I think it would be a good experience for the child to help Joe. Anyway, the boy has to begin somewhere."

Catherine and Benny were not so sure about this new arrangement. They silently exchanged looks—funny grimacing faces, and exaggerating rolling eyes.

Almost one month later, Aunt Geraldine and Floyd arrived in the wagon that Father had sent to pick them up in Rochester. Floyd was all decked out in a pristine pressed white shirt. He struck Benny as an undersized child with a bright innocent face.

"Want to see where your room is?" Benny asked. Floyd's clear blue eyes sparkled as he happily tagged three steps behind his older cousin. He had to run just to keep up the pace.

Father carried the suitcases as the workers helped unload from the wagon two heavy steamer trunks that could barely be maneuvered because of the bulk and weight. The men rolled and pushed the steamer trunks into the back entrance of the house, scraping the walls. Finally, the luggage was deposited in the two rooms that stood behind the playroom, rooms that had been prepared as small quarters for the new additions to the Treadwell family.

"Mother look, we have our own place here," Floyd excitedly called out, running from the water closet to the bedroom to the small parlor. Aunt Geraldine appeared distressed and uncomfortable. When she hugged her sister Elizabeth, she kept a safe arms distance from her. Geraldine's stiff composure visibly disclosed the fact that she lacked a warm spirit. Benny glanced at Catherine and raised one eyebrow, signaling their biggest fear, that Geraldine was not going to run the household with the warmth and grace that their grandmother had. Regardless of her short temper and lack of patience, Grandma always loved the children and tried to do what was best for them.

"C'mon Floyd, I'll show you my old tree fort I built when I was about your age." Floyd ran outside following Benny's heels. The rear door banged shut behind them and Geraldine grimaced.

Benny pulled Floyd up by his skinny arms onto the ledge of the tree fort. It was obvious by the look on Floyd's face that the height of the tree frightened the boy. Floyd gingerly peeked over the edge of the wooden platform.

"Now you can take over, I have so much other stuff to do now; I haven't had time to play here for over three years."

Floyd, overwhelmed by his cousin's generosity, carefully surveyed the small area. He propped open a side window to peek out of the tree fort. Trouble was Floyd leaned over so far to see how high they were that Benny had to rescue him by tugging on his pant waist.

"Whoa boy! Don't go doing that, you'll damn fall flat on your head, and according to my father, I'll be to blame and get my ass whipped."

After inspecting every corner of the fort, the first words Floyd said to Benny were, "Can I make some changes?"

"Only if I approve of them first." Benny's face broke into a grin. *This kid is kinda' smart.* "What changes would you make anyway? I thought it was perfect myself."

"Well, the first thing I need is a higher ladder so I can get up here without you having to pull me up."

*The kid, though puny was cute.* Affectionately, Benny tousled Floyd's sandy colored head of hair.

"Can't refuse that."

Floyd officially became the new caretaker of the tree fort that Benny temporarily abandoned. Once again the valley filled with the sounds of a pounding hammer coming from the overgrown tree as if a renewal of a summer ritual.

It was obvious to everyone that Floyd idolized his older cousin, and that Aunt Geraldine disapproved of the close relationship. She appeared sometimes green with envy that her son would shower so much attention on such a boisterous, unruly, and primitive boy. Floyd was quickly indoctrinated into becoming a proper woodsman, setting traps, hunting deer, learning to shoot. Benny took him on an overnight trip to visit one of the many logging camps. They toured the camps that harvested hardwoods, birches, and maples along with the inevitable white pine.

Floyd's soft little white hands soon weathered, and his frail body showed signs of maturity and strength. Floyd, third in the pecking order behind Benny and Joe, was instructed to do all the dirty work like gutting the wild game they trapped and cleaning the fish they caught. Floyd learned to set up a lean-to, this after carrying in a good amount of gear to the camp. He also learned to skin the pelts they had trapped. Some nights the boys would come in for dinner stinking to high heaven of bear grease, beaver pelts, and skunk essence. Aunt Geraldine oftentimes failed to recognize that Floyd was the same sweet child who she had labored fifteen hours to birth.

In the beginning of fall, the small boy bundled into several stiff layers of sweaters and woolen shirts, thrilled that Benny would allow him to tag along into the forest to hunt. Benny patiently taught his cousin compass skills, how to memorize the land, and path markers to enable a safe return after an excursion.

This day, Benny climbed a tree and waited silently while Joe and Floyd entered the forest down the road by the sandpit. The duo was to noisily tramp through the trees and flush the deer into Benny's path. Though a light dusting of snow insulated the ground, Benny could hear the commotion from a distance. When he caught sight of a deer running toward him, he aimed and shot the deer dead. The boys bagged their trophy and together they dragged it clear out of the woods. The deer was large enough to feed the crew and their family that night— a delicious and tender venison stew.

With all the changes in his life, Benny failed to notice that several nights his mother began to arrive home later than usual. Aunt Geraldine kept his mother's dinner, covered with a pot top, on the back of the stove. One morning, when Benny and Floyd came to breakfast before school, Benny noticed his mother's dinner had remained untouched, the dish still on the stove. After school that day, he was surprised to find his mother at home, which was unusual since it was midday. Benny noticed she was hunched over, sitting alone in the breakfast room with her housecoat on, and her face red and swollen. She apparently was not feeling well. After his initial greeting, Benny tip-toed around her making sure to stay out of her way. He thought maybe her temper might be short feeling as bad as she looked. He noticed Aunt Geraldine had baked some iced cookies, so he changed his clothes quickly, stuffed a handful of cookies into his pant pocket, and escaped to the barn.

Gossip quickly spread—conversations across fences, over cups of hot tea, and glasses of whiskey and beer—that old Benjamin finally got what he deserved. No other man within the township had allowed his wife a career in lieu of caring for a family. Yes, he finally got what he deserved for being so pompous and wealthy, and the way he shoved his success down everyone's throat. The gossipmongers did not bother to blame Elizabeth for her indiscretions, they blamed her husband.

In quiet whispers, the story unveiled that early one afternoon a couple of months earlier a motor bike with a sidecar pulled into the mill yard. The young man who dismounted was dressed in leather gear from head to foot and wore an aviator type helmet and goggles. He had come from Brasher Falls to special order wainscoting and heavy beams for his home. The sparks that crossed between Elizabeth and this young man were evident, some employees even left early for the day in pure disgust. Fact is that even though Elizabeth was rapidly approaching middle age, it was obvious she was still a handsome and captivating woman. Tongues started to wag when she would be indisposed and unavailable during the middle of the workday. Funny thing was as suddenly as the biker appeared one day, he vanished and was never seen around again. As gossip slowly died down, Benny's mother was now home more often than not, though her facial expression was pained, and the gleam missing from her dark eyes.

Occasionally, Benny would pass her locked bedroom door and hear her sobbing. It became apparent to him that something died inside of her, but her physical body still lived, moved, and breathed. She still managed to find some small solace in involving herself in the planning of community events and lawn parties. She would conspicuously arrive looking fashionable in elaborate French silk dresses, but an air of gloomy detachment surrounded her demeanor.

# Benny Treadwell
# The Confrontation

▼

"Don't forget to take along your skating lanterns," Aunt Geraldine called down onto the dark and forbidden basement where Benny and Floyd sat on the cold earth floor rubbing bear grease into the leather of their ice skates.

"I hope we find a good patch of ice," Floyd said wistfully.

"Grab that shovel and broom," Benny ordered Floyd, who quickly responded by lugging the tools up the steps, his skates tied together and tossed over one shoulder and two lanterns barely hanging from his small curled fingers.

"Anything else we need?" Floyd asked.

Benny was in his element organizing the expedition for the first skate of the season.

"Well, I do think we have it all," Benny said, patting the flap pocket on his shirt checking to be sure he had remembered a good supply of wooden matches.

The pond was a short brisk walk from their house. The bright moon overhead illuminated the snow. It took only a few steps before both boys had to sniffle, their noses drippy wet, and cheeks quickly turning the color of ripe cherries.

"When we get back later, I have a surprise for you," Benny said.

Floyd knew that sounded like trouble.

"I happened to find two cigars sitting all alone looking kinda' lonely on my father's desk. I thought we can smoke them later, that's if you're not too scared."

Floyd rolled his eyes.

"I hid them yesterday in the tree fort. You must have found my secret hiding place by now."

Floyd shook his head. He was breathing heavy now because the gear was becoming heavier by the moment. Benny finally relented and relieved Floyd of some of his burden.

"Did you find the loose board in the floor? Years ago, I painted the inside with tar and it's still weather tight. Never know when you need to hide something special."

"Guess you thought about everything." Floyd said.

"That's why I brought along extra matches."

"What if my mother finds out?"

"Your mother won't find out, sissy boy, unless you tell her."

"You always get me into trouble with her."

"Don't worry about nuttin', Cuz. Nobody will find out. You sure won't catch me ratting on you."

They walked along in silence, repeatedly." wiping their cold, drippy nose with their coat sleeves. Floyd was dreading getting caught smoking his uncle Benjamin's cigars.

"Do you think the pond is frozen solid enough?" Floyd asked, running ahead to the edge where during the summer they would launch their canoe.

Benny took the snow shovel and began to clear a small patch of ice. "Follow behind me with the broom and clear away the loose snow." he instructed Floyd as he watched him step gingerly along the edge of the frozen pond.

"We definitely have enough ice for tonight."

The pond area was roughly about twenty square feet. The two boys sat on a snow shelf to lace their skates.

"My ankles always hurt real bad after the first time I skate," Floyd complained.

"That's because my little cuz has weak ankle muscles," Benny teased.

Floyd picked up a huge rock of frozen snow and hurled it in Benny's general direction.

"Looks like you'll be sweeping while I am skating," Benny said, pointing to the mess the misdirected ball of snow had made.

Floyd dutifully picked up the broom and cleared away the loose snow that had messed up the ice. They lit the oil lanterns and placed them strategically on opposite sides of the skating area.

"Race you," Benny said as he skated away from Floyd. At the end of the ice pond, Benny turned and saw Floyd flat on his back.

"I banged the back of my head really hard," he cried, tears welling into pools. He stifled the tears because he did not want to be embarrassed and cry in front of his cousin. He wiped his face and eyes with his mittens.

"You'll live," Benny said, reaching down to help Floyd back to his feet

"You keep trying to race with me, but you're just not big enough, I guess. Try to skate around to get your balance, and then we'll race again after you warm up."

Floyd leisurely skated around in small circles all the while massaging the lump that had formed on the back of his head.

"Now, I can race you," he said, taking off.

Benny laughed.

"Cuz, you don't stand a chance, let's go."

Benny raced along leaving Floyd far behind.

Their ears picked up the sound of the La Due brothers talking in the distance. As the brothers approached the newly formed skating area, they stopped to chat.

"What are you two doing out so late?" Benny asked.

"We wanted to see what trouble you cousins were getting into tonight," one of the La Due brothers quipped.

"Bet you just waited to see if we cleared the ice. Probably were spying on us 'til we finished all the work of cleaning the ice pond."

"Somethin' akin to that. Is there a problem with being efficient?" the older brother asked as he sat down to lace up his skates.

"No problem just thought it was worth mentioning. You are both welcome to skate along with us," Benny said, deciding to lean toward diplomacy.

After Floyd had fallen for the sixth or seventh time, he finally crawled to a far corner of the ice.

"Come on, Cuz, this place is too crowded. Let's head home for something warm. Everyone is expecting us back anyway," Benny said.

"I don't rightly think I could have fallen one more time, my rump is sore." Floyd confessed. He removed his skates and ran in the direction of the tree fort. Benny removed his skates, gathered the oil lanterns, and the two of them scampered up the wooden ladder rungs, Benny in the lead.

"I know, I think your brains were ready to spill out of your ears, boy."

"I think so too." Floyd answered innocently.

"We can light one of the oil lamps here," said Benny, pointing to a space on the tree fort floor.

"Don't light nuttin'," Floyd pleaded. "My mother has an eagle eye and will notice the light from the house."

They propped themselves against the wooden boards after undoing their scarves and discarding their hats and mittens.

"Listen," Floyd said, his ear pushed up hard against the cold wood.

They both became acutely alert and listened carefully. Muffled voices floated on the crisp air.

"It's my mother and father," Benny whispered. Both boys sat perfectly still in fear of being discovered. Floyd's eyes were wide in fright, and he tried to act brave.

"I know what you have done." It was Benny's mother speaking, her voice filled with chilling animosity.

"You don't know anything at all," his father answered in his *know it all* voice.

Mother began to cry, sobbing softly, her voice becoming throaty and guttural.

"I know, Benjamin, I know everything. I should leave you for what you have done," she continued to sob.

Father answered, speaking slowly, enunciating each word carefully.

"Elizabeth, you won't leave, you cannot leave me. You are too comfortable with the life I have given you. And the children, what about the children? You know as God is my witness you will never be allowed to see them again."

She began crying louder now, more distinctly.

"The crime I committed is not comparable to the offensive and wicked act you willingly participated in."

Floyd started to speak, but Benny put his finger over his lips. "Shhhhush," he whispered.

"I am aware of what you refuse to acknowledge. That fact is that everyone knows, the whole town knows."

Elizabeth was crying hysterically now, barely able to speak through her heaving sobs.

"No," Father said, as if further provoking her pain. "Everyone knows what *you* have done. I did nothing but mend the hole in the dike. The problem is over. Besides, I do believe if anyone professes to think they know what I did, they may be in full agreement of the solution."

The boys positioned themselves in front of a large knothole and peered out. They could barely make out the two figures below. The moonlight provided a faint blue light over the two, standing among the dark shadows of the trees.

"You are an insane monster!" Her voice was filled with fury and hate.

"I hope one day your son discovers the real person you have become. Everybody thinks you to be a great man. They think you have scruples, only I know the truth."

"Hush, Elizabeth, the workers will hear." He took hold of her shoulders and began to shake her violently.

"Do you really believe I care who knows the truth about me?" she asked.

"You care, you would care Elizabeth. You would care if the Treadwell name were tarnished. You already know we would have to leave here. You would care if *my lady* had to leave the empire I built for you. The pampered comfort you enjoy so very much."

She was crying now in affirmation of his cruel words.

He began to stroke her hair. "Now, let's both go inside and have our supper."

"How can you behave so toward me?"

"I can do whatever I have to do," he answered sternly.

"Good!" she said, and violently released herself from his grasp. She turned and headed defiantly toward the house, they distinctly could hear the sound of the snow crunching under the heels of her high boots.

"Then I shall do what I shall have to do," she answered firmly from over her shoulder.

"Don't ever speak to me about this again," he said in a voice filled with the finality of his words.

She had already taken ten strides when she halted in her tracks. She turned bravely to face him.

"You will never hear of this again from my lips," she said, her eyes blazing pure hatred.

She reached the rear doorway of the house and entered the kitchen. The boys watched transfixed, as Benny's father sat down on a boulder clear of snow. He deliberately reached into his pocket and pulled out a fresh cigar, wet the tip, and lit it. He sat quietly staring into the back of the house and gazing blindly up at the moon, puffs of smoke gathering about his ears.

"I'm cold," the small boy whispered, distracting Benny.

"Be quiet," he said as he watched his father.

"What's going on anyway?"

"I don't know, but if you don't shut up, the shit will be beat out of our hides when we get caught."

There was silence. Benny peeked through the knothole again. His father was still sitting in the same position, silently puffing the cigar he held between his clenched teeth. His hands casually folded on his lap.

"We have to stay quiet while my father finishes his smoke," he whispered in Floyd's ear. The younger boy was beginning to shiver. He had bundled the scarf thick around his neck and was hugging himself for warmth.

When Benny peered again through the knothole searching for his father, he noticed he was gone. Benny thought he heard the latch fall on the back door lock.

"We can go now." He pulled Floyd to his feet, dragged him to the ladder, and pushed him ahead.

"Don't you ever tell anyone what we heard tonight, you hear?"

Floyd nodded, not really grasping the situation, but understanding that something bad had happened.

"I promise, Benny. Let's go inside now. I'm really getting scared."

The boys climbed down the ladder and crept around to the front of the house, and quickly forgot all about the two cigars in the tree fort.

# THE DREAM

▼

Cammi had perfected her packing technique to the point that the clothes were folded in the suitcases three weeks before the family's scheduled departure. Michael reviewed his work schedule in order for Ron to complete certain deadlines. Ron was now working with Michael two days each week to make some extra money. Cammi was so busy during this time she would only touch her head to the pillow, and she went out like a light. One particular night though she tossed and turned, unable to get comfortable, her mind buzzing along a million miles a minute, reviewing what she had packed and what she still needed to buy for the trip. She dozed off once and then awoke fitfully in the middle of the night. An unknown anxiety gripped her gut and tightened her insides for a reason she could not explain. Then she snuggled into just the right position and dropped off into a deep sleep.

She was immersed in a heavy wet fog. Drops of water from the tall treetops fell onto a thick carpet of decomposing leaves under her feet. She was jogging barefoot through the heavy brush, low ferns tickling her ankles. She sensed it was important to keep pace with the small deer running ahead of her. The deer stopped abruptly, and then turned to watch her, beckoning her to follow. The deer's eyes blazed red fire as it telepathically persuaded her to continue. When the deer turned to run again, it was as though two red headlights illuminated the path ahead, projecting a smoky redness into the depths of the fog.

Cammi peered over her shoulder at the forbidding darkness closing in behind her. She felt the power of an unknown entity that lay hidden in that darkness push her ever forward. A peculiar misshapen moon shone in the distance surrounded by wisps of smoke that formed strange designs. The shapes constantly moved. She caught a glimpse of illuminated reflections shimmering on the horizon.

She began to tire. Panting, she opened her mouth wide, gasped for air, and sucked in as much as her lungs could hold. A small clearing lay ahead. A twinkling glow from candles became distinguishable. The tiny rays flickered on the boughs of the pine forest in front of her. She stopped at the outer edge of the forest and leaned her back against a huge tree. Pinecones littered the ground, and up ahead she saw a barren mound of dirt. She discovered the deer had disappeared. She realized she was alone. Her heavy breathing created clouds of icy particles as she made her way into the open clearing.

Suddenly a large house with many windows and gables loomed in her path halting any further advance. The sight of it terrified her. She screamed. The moonlight shone a sickening blue tinge on the siding. All the windows appeared opaque. Light suddenly emanated from the front door now ablaze with fingers of luminous color. Tiny circular lights danced on the dusting of snow that had magically appeared on a front lawn. Shivering from the sudden frigid air, she climbed the three stone steps to peer into the glass front doors.

The scene was incongruous to her expectations. Children sat cross-legged in front of a blazing fireplace, the ornate mantel adorned in thick festive colored garland. The children were all girls, and they all wore pink and yellow ribbons in their hair. They clapped merrily and chattered. Cammi saw two boys hanging back from the group. They were pointing, whispering, and laughing at the girls.

Abruptly, the girls stopped chattering. They all turned their heads and gazed at Cammi's face peering through the doorway window. Suddenly, and without warning, the group jumped up and scampered through a doorway to the right of the fireplace. Cammi could hear them giggling in a very excited and happy way. The front doorknob turned as if from an invisible hand and the door creaked and swung open. Cautiously, she entered the room and quickly headed toward the doorway through which the children had disappeared.

There she found a tight narrow hallway that enclosed a long flight of stairs. Upstairs, the sound of giggling children beckoned her. During her agonizingly slow ascent up the stairs, she envisioned an unseen force guiding her. Shivers of fear traveled up her spine with each step.

When she reached the top landing, a sudden silence engulfed her. She turned left, compelled to enter a large room filled with sinister emptiness. She felt a blanket of ice wrap around her. Her senses honed sharp as she took in every miniscule detail of her surroundings. She noticed flowerpots neatly arranged along the inside windowsill. Red potted geraniums with a musty scent covered the full length of both sills. For just a moment, a flicker of familiarity shot through her. Intense fear tightened its grip, starting in her lower intestine and rising into her stomach. Nauseous and confused, she was aware that she vaguely recognized her surroundings. Still, her memory would not release further information, though she consciously realized she knew the layout of the upper floors and the exact location of each room below.

Squinting in the darkness, she carefully surveyed the rest of the room. In one corner, she noticed a pair of bib jeans and large boots lumped on the floor. Red suspenders hung over a hook mounted outside the closet, and a sickening sweet smell of cigar smoke permeated the room. She heard faint voices from outside and below. She went to the window to investigate and noticed a group of men talking, animatedly tossing their hands into the air, one voice indistinguishable from the others. When she pressed her face to the window to get a better view, one of the men raised his pale, deeply lined face toward her.

He wore a union soldier's blue uniform. The shiny gold buttons on the tunic reflected the moonlight. His eyes locked on her. She felt her throat constrict in a strangling grip of fear. Ever so slowly, he raised both arms as if to embrace her. His fingers stretched an unnatural length in an attempt to reach her. His mouth voiced silent words. She tried to read his lips. She struggled to open the window, but it would not budge. The soldier's lips moved urgently. He wanted her to understand his words.

*What does he want with me?*

In transfixed amazement, she became cognizant of the meaning of the unheard words. The message started in her mind as a whisper and grew until the words screamed inside her head.

*They want you back!*

She recoiled in horror. The soldier's frightening stare drew her in. Shivers rippled through her body. She felt a sudden cold draft. She tried to scream, but was locked in the malevolent nature of his wild look.

She shook herself free from his penetrating gaze and turned to run. In front of her stood a woman dressed in black. The woman's eyebrows arched quizzically as she gazed mournfully into Cammi's eyes. Cammi tried hard to remember the woman's name, to call out to her, to ask her *why*. Then, as though offended, the woman turned away in a huff, and lifting her dress skirts, sauntered out of the room. As she disappeared down the hallway, the rustling of each layer of taffeta made an exaggerated, grating sound.

Cammi tried to run back down the stairs, but suddenly a black wall halted her advance. In the distance, she could hear sounds of the children laughing insanely. Time stopped. Pure terror gripped her mind. She was trapped in the room. The house seemed to take on a life of its own. A sound emanated from the wall. It suddenly reached a deafening pitch, heaving the wall outward with each crushing beat.

*A heartbeat?*

Drowning out all other sound, the beat became louder still. Cammi pushed her body up against the monster wall and felt the surge of each beat in her effort to escape. When she saw she could not budge the wall, she started to claw at it with her fingertips. Starting at the top of the wall, blood oozed from each crevice, running slimy in thick gobs to the floor. In a gooey mess, it coagulated in puddles under her feet. Terror encased her. Her legs felt heavy as if mired in mud. Gurgling noises escaped from her throat as she clawed at the wall. She realized her feet felt warm and wet. She looked down to see her ankles deep in coagulated blood. Her scream pierced the air. Her eyes shot open.

She awoke in a paralyzed state of terror.

*Shit! What a friggin' dream!*

She shot out from under the sheets. Her heart pounded against her rib cage. She gasped for air as she labored to remove the fear that encased her cold clammy body. She ran to the safety of her own bathroom sink and splashed water on her face to rid her mind of the cloak of terror that still held its grip. She shook her head and raised her eyes to the mirror. Bright eyes with glowing flames replaced her own eyes, a reflection of his eyes, and the soldier from her dream. Horrified, her mouth gaped as the eyes slowly faded and were replaced by her own. She laughed nervously thinking, *that was probably the worst dream of my entire life.*

She sat on the toilet and took deep breaths to calm her nerves and purge the frightening thoughts from her brain. She did not have the nerve to climb back under the covers for fear the dream would begin again. She sat still, her mind turning round and round reliving the dream as if a movie. She was confused over what part of the dream, if any, was reality. There was the chilling realization that some parts of the dream lay hidden in the recesses of her mind. She somehow grasped that this was the beginning of a long journey with no end. It took a long time for her heart to settle down, to beat quietly again. Only then did she begin to feel more like herself. Reluctantly, she returned to bed.

Michael was sound asleep, breathing heavy. A freight train would not have roused him tonight, she thought, good thing he did not hear me.

She lay quietly under the covers, thinking about the Ouija board experience years ago and wondering if it had any correlation with her dream tonight. She closed her eyes. A vision of the house flashed alive again. She spent the remaining hours until dawn with her eyes open and listening to her husband breathing. His steady breaths lulled her into another dimension where she fought to focus on the vacation trip ahead.

Regrettably, the children were up early, hungry, and demanding breakfast. Cammi dragged herself around the kitchen and managed to make pancakes.

That evening, in submissive exhaustion, she fell asleep soon after bathing the girls.

Michael put the children to bed. He gently covered his wife with a blanket after noticing that she had been running double duty the last few weeks.

He was only slightly aware that lately Cammi's temper was short. Darker than normal circles under her eyes led him to believe her allergies were flaring up. He quietly tiptoed from the bedroom to watch late night television, but she was so tired she would not have heard him any way.

Three weeks passed quickly. Cammi was so occupied with the activities involved with the trip she was able to put the disturbing visions from the dream behind her. Finally, all the floors were mopped, and the bathroom was scrubbed until the tile glistened. Leftovers were cleared from the refrigerator, the washing machine had a workout, and the overstuffed suitcases were locked shut.

"How many more days until we leave, Mommy?" Renee asked that question several times a day. If Jenna were anywhere around, she would rattle off the exact time to the precise minute. Each girl had organized their backpacks, randomly stuffed with coloring books, games, and books to read. Small boxes of animal crackers, candies, and snacks caused the front pockets to bulge.

Michael phoned. "You've probably been busy all day, so I ordered pizza for dinner. I'll pick it up on my way home tonight."

"Oh, thanks, honey. I have everything ready. All you have left to do is pack the car. How are things going with Ron? Is he ready to take over and finish the tile work on the Heinrich job?"

"Yeah, he took a couple of vacation days off with the department, so he'll be fine. The kids must be excited for tonight. I sure am, can hardly wait until tonight. I never thought an eight-hour car trip with two kids could excite me so much."

"Most likely because we are in desperate need to get away. Hope I don't need a vacation from *this* vacation when we get back. The kids' suitcases are packed solid, and we may need to buy a new washing machine."

"Don't go worrying your little head about that, there is still a couple of bucks left over from our windfall. Unless we spend it all on this trip, we're still okay."

"How about shooting to leave about nine? This way the girls can bed down in the back with a couple of blankets and sleep."

"Sounds perfect to me, we can tune into the old doo-wop on the radio and sing our way all the way north."

"Shu doopie scuby doo. I love you. Just get your body home and let's leave!"

At 9:30 they pulled out of the driveway, the back of the car weighted down by the suitcases and the children.

"I can't believe we're really on our way," Cammi said.

Michael was humming. "I know, me also. I'm really glad we used the money we won for the car and the trip, otherwise, we would have just bought something stupid. Like something we really needed, and it would be all gone by now."

"That's what I love about you, your sense of practical money spending."

Cammi reached for a thermos of coffee and carefully poured some into the thermos cap.

"Want some? It's going to be a long drive."

"Sure." Michael reached over and carefully raised the cup to his lips.

"I heard you up tossing and turning the last couple of weeks. Is everything okay? I noticed you haven't been sleeping so well."

Cammi felt the muscles in her stomach constrict.

"Just excited," she lied. "But now that we're on our way, I can relax." She snuggled her head into just the perfect place on his shoulder. Michael took the wheel in one hand and put his arm around her.

"Let's pretend this is the old '57 Ford we used to drive to school," he said.

They drove in silence for an hour or so. "In the Still of the Night" was playing in the background, and Michael was humming along. Cammi felt herself begin to doze off.

Suddenly, in her mind, she was walking up the dark stairway of *that house* again. Her brain was playing tricks on her. She did not want to remember, not now, not during the vacation she had looked so forward to. She reached to turn off the radio. Michael groaned.

"What'd you go and do that for?"

"What do you want to do when we first get there?" she asked, diverting his attention.

"Well now, we could go directly to Santa's Workshop, or we could first stop at the cabin we've rented. Maybe get a little shuteye. Or," he added jovially, "we could fool around a little."

Cammi ignored his remark. "I really don't think we are going to be able to get much sleep, the children will be so excited when we finally arrive."

They reached the cabin eight and a half hours later. It was early dawn and the sun sparkled through the trees casting long summer shadows on the highway. A heavy scent of pine penetrated the dew-filled air.

"This must be it, 104 Pine Echo Circle." Cammi said.

They both got out of the car and ran as fast as they could to see which one would reach the cabin door first. Michael's back was stiff from driving, so Cammi arrived first. Her outstretched hand was a signal to Michael to give her the key sent to them through the mail.

"Do you want to go in first, madam?" Michael smiled.

She grabbed the key from his hand and quickly unlocked the door.

"Wow! This is gorgeous," she said, inspecting every nook and cranny. She ran up the stairs to the loft that circled around the downstairs living room paneled in rustic knotty pine. The living room had a full stone fireplace. A caramel colored leather sofa faced the fireplace. Michael raised his eyebrows when he first saw the couch and motioned to Cammi as if to say, *too bad the kids are with us.*

"They only needed to put a bear skin rug on the floor to complete the look," she said.

After moving in all the luggage and supplies, they carried in each child, still asleep, and laid them on a separate bunk bed on the second level.

"Who can sleep now?" Michael said, and walked outside to the porch.

He made himself comfortable in one of the four Adirondack chairs. Hands folded across his belly, he propped his legs up on the low porch wall that wrapped around the exterior of the cabin.

Cammi wrapped herself inside a woolen blanket from the headrest of the sofa. She shivered when she went outside and snuggled up into a chair closest to Michael.

"Listen," she said. The only sound breaking the silence of the beautiful dawn was the chirping of birds flitting back and forth from the trees to the lawn.

"How about you take the kids to Santa's Workshop and I stay here?" Michael asked pleadingly.

They held hands and enjoyed the fresh morning air. They admired the extraordinary landscape and felt peaceful. Somewhere in the distance, they heard a rooster crow and they smiled. An Adirondack morning had greeted the Fanelli family. It was love at first sight.

# THE MOVE

▼

A demonstration by the glass blower in his small cottage caught Michael's interest. By the third day of their vacation, the family had visited Santa's Workshop twice and Land of Make Believe once. This was Michael's third visit to this glass shop. The colors and forms created by the master glass blower intrigued him. Every inch of the store contained miniscule blown glass collectibles and very expensive colored vases. The nature of this shop required strict adult supervision to keep little hands from touching and destroying the merchandise. Renee had fallen asleep propped upon Michael's shoulders. Even though she had the best view she had been undoubtedly bored.

Jenna tugged at her mother's shirt for another ice cream until Cammi finally relented. They left together and headed straight to the ice cream maker's tiny cottage where they served delicious soft ice cream in a waffle cone with sprinkles.

Jenna skipped along behind Cammi as they made their way back to Michael. The glass blower demonstration had concluded, and they found Michael engrossed in serious conversation with a stranger. The man held a clipboard in one hand and was writing rapidly as Michael spoke.

"What's the matter, honey?" she asked.

Michael shooed her away "I'll talk to you about it later."

He then continued his conversation with the man.

Cammi took Jenna with her to sit on a park bench. There she relaxed in full sunlight, tousled her hair, and enjoyed a spectacular view of the mountains.

When Michael approached, his boyish expression mirrored that of a small child with a stupendous surprise.

"Guess who that man is?" he began.

"Go on, I know you're going to tell me whether I want to know or not."

"Well, after the glass demonstration, the glass blower introduced me to that man over there, Jason Perido. Jason is supervising new additions and renovation work on these cottages that must be completed within three years. The cottages are the original buildings from years ago. Obviously, the shop merchants have outgrown their quarters."

"And?" Cammi asked quizzically, wondering what Michael was going to say next.

"I overheard the glass blower complain about how small and tight the space is in his shop. So, I arranged for their corporate office to send specs and architect plans to us ... at home. I really want to bid for this job."

"And move here?" Cammi's voice was filled with animated surprise.

"I thought, what the hell. It's worth a chance, maybe they'll accept our bid, and we can become year-round Adirondack residents."

Cammi threw her arms around Michael.

"You always manage to surprise me. I am so excited! I would love it. We all would love it if it really happened." She looked down at Jenna sitting next to her. Jenna's face and chin was covered with ice cream. Cammi leaned over to wipe her face clean.

"I'm behind you, Michael; as always, one hundred percent. I'll type the estimate the minute we get home. I've been boning up on my secretarial skills, thanks to you."

Cammi beamed all afternoon, although she still had many questions. But, being adventurous, she knew that change would be a good thing as long as the family remained together.

Later in the day, they drove to the summit of Whiteface Mountain. They walked the pathway and then climbed the steps to the highest point at 4,386 feet. Standing atop the summit, exposed to every earthly element, Cammi found the scenery extraordinary. The melodic sound of the wind could almost be mistaken for the howl of a wolf; gusting sometimes with such strength it seemed to strip her of her clothes. With an iron grasp on her family, viewing the lush panorama below, she felt as though they had found *their place*. She looked at Michael, and he smiled back in an unspoken agreement that they would willingly be able to start a new life here in this majestically beautiful part of the country. After a whirlwind nine-day vacation, they left the Adirondack area armed with a local phone book the cabin office had supplied. They were ready to live their shared dream and anxious to make plans for a new, exciting life.

Ever resourceful, Cammi had set aside a special notebook crammed with ideas and checklists of people to contact in the Adirondack area.

"Do you really think we can swing this?" Michael asked Cammi sitting in the passenger side of the car during their drive home.

"Well," she answered, "we cannot do any worse monetarily. At this point, from what we have seen, it appears to be cheaper to live up here."

"What do you suppose your parents will think?"

"My mother might not ever forgive me."

"Guess she'll have to get used to the idea," Michael answered, slightly annoyed. "I know we'll enjoy it here. It will undoubtedly be an experience of a lifetime for us."

"Wonder how much snow they get up here."

"Probably from our Long Island perspective, we'll see lots of ice and snow," Michael said. "Some guy I met at Dairy Queen told me sometimes the snow banks halfway up the electric poles."

"Get out of here! Sounds like we better buy skis for each of us," she teased.

"And does it really get a whole bunch colder than Long Island during the winter?"

"Well," he tried to soften the blow, "the temperature does drop below the zero mark during the winter months. Don't forget the elevation is so much higher, and we are eight hours farther north."

"How would you like to move here?" she playfully asked the girls sitting in the backseat of the car.

A loud, "Yes, hooray!" confirmed their answer.

The drive home seemed much quicker than the drive north. Everyone happily chattered, and no one slept. It was almost a done deal, the move up north, as though it had become an accepted fact.

About a hundred miles from Long Island, Michael turned to Cammi."Do you really think it will work, baby? I mean what if I don't get the bid on the job."

"At this point, we're moving anyway," her voice was steady and sure.

"We're going to make it work together. I'm convinced we can make a good living up here. You'll have to first get your general contractor's license, and then you can hang your shingle up in front of our brand new log cabin home. The best part of the deal is you have a built-in office manager."

"I've always wanted to start my own enterprise. This is a good chance for me."

"And I've always wanted to sit in the lap of my employer," Cammi said. "You know, take dictation and all."

Michael grinned.

They arrived home on Long Island late Sunday afternoon. Six weeks later, Michael received a letter accepting his bid for construction at Santa's Workshop.

Cammi telephoned Lucille, her close friend and Michael's sister, with the news about their unexpected and spontaneous move north.

"You guys make up your minds awfully quick," Lucille said.

"Well, your brother is a spontaneous kinda' guy."

"And you? How are you with this?"

"Well, while I was up there, I was drawn into the excitement of it all. But now that it's a reality, it's a little scary."

"Scary? How do you mean?"

"Well, lately I have had some weird dreams. There's something I can't put my finger on. Problem is, I love Michael, and I want to be supportive."

"Have you talked with him about this?"

"No, not yet. There are some things I can't tell him about."

"Mr. Macho at it again?"

"That's what I like about you Lou, you know the real guy nobody else sees."

"Yup, grew up with it, I should know it by now," Lucille said.

"Usually I'm more complicated than Michael reads into."

"Sounds like the rest of the population."

"Yeah, but they don't have to live with Michael, I do."

After they broke the news to the rest of the family, Cammi's mother refused to believe they could do something as stupid as to move so far away from everyone in the family. Ron and Marie were most surprised at the unexpected news. Marie actually broke down at the prospect of losing her closest friend.

"Here we've gotten so close," Marie sobbed. "But I really do believe it's going to be a good move for you, even though I will miss you a lot."

"It will be a good change. It's just so beautiful there, and I am so ready for a change."

"I've never been so far north," Marie said. "Ron hasn't taken me any farther than Hackensack, New Jersey." They giggled together and ended up crying.

Two weeks later, Jenna and Renee happily left for a sleepover at Aunt Lucille's house. This allowed time for Michael and Cammi to drive upstate to secure a rental on a home. They also had an appointment to sign the contract for the scheduled construction work. Knowing exactly what she was looking for; Cammi had set up phone appointments through an agency for rental homes. By the end of the weekend, they had signed a contract for the construction job, and secured a home rental agreement for a year.

The rental house was located in an awesome location situated on Beaver Ridge, overlooking the mountains. Huge red maples grew along the top of the ridge, and the large front windows framed an exquisite view of the west side of Whiteface Mountain. Their nearest neighbor was a half mile away. It was a long trek into Saranac Lake to shop, and Wilmington was even a little farther. At least they did not have to worry about the traffic jams like they did on Long Island. Michael did have one realistic concern. The driveway from the rental house sloped very steeply down to meet the highway.

"How the hell am I going to clear the snow off this monster driveway? We just might have to invest in a snow blower."

The realtor had heard his concern and said, "Don't you worry; we have a neighbor here who comes around during every big snowstorm. He works for the town, and thankfully, he drives the town vehicles, so he just plows out all his neighbors. I'm sure he'd do that for you folks too."

The realtor had also been aware that Cammi was gawking at the magnificent, panoramic view of the mountains.

"On a clear day, honey, you can easily see the tower on top of that mountain," the realtor had said. "Some days though, you're going to see that mountain look fierce, turn red and purple according to the weather and the sunlight. You'd better hunker down when she turns black, 'cause you're going to get some real serious snow soon afterward. But just wait until the glorious moment when you see it turn gold as the sun goes down; it's like you died and went to heaven."

This day it was crisp and clear. The mountain was mauve and gray with sunlight reflecting off small bodies of water around the peak area, glistening like a diamond in the sky.

The owners of the newly rented property were an older couple who had spent their entire adult lives in their home raising a large family. Hoping one day to retire and raise a few pigs, unfortunately the old man was diagnosed with an incurable bone cancer. Upon hearing this life altering news, the couple decided to invest in a comfortable, well-equipped motor home. The object was to take off for a year or so, visit their children, and drive to points yet unknown. The doctors had given him eighteen months, maybe two years. The couple found comfort that such a nice family would care for their beloved home while they were traveling. Even though they knew this was their last trip, they were happy that their property would be in good hands.

Cammi learned later that after the initial meeting and interview with Michael, the older couple had gone upstairs to their bedroom. There they lay down together in bed believing fate had led Cammi and Michael to their doorstep.

Cammi knew that once they arrived back on Long Island, the sixty days remaining to coordinate and prepare for such a long distance move would be overwhelming. She had reams of notes detailing the parties that needed to be informed of the move; what had to be shut off and when. She made appointments. She packed boxes and labeled cartons with different colored tape so the boxes would be placed in the appropriate rooms. Cheerfully, she announced to everyone she knew that she and her family were leaving *the rat race* behind and starting all over in an exciting new environment.

Ron offered to drive the rental truck upstate, and then return it after the move. The neighbors threw a surprise going-away party, and then they all pitched in to help load the rental truck. After the ramp was lowered an army of friends packed the Fanelli family belongings into it. The station wagon was packed solid. Only small cramped spaces remained for the children. The moment had finally arrived, and they were ready to roll. Full of anticipation and some regrets, the Fanelli family waved good-bye to the suburbs and again headed north.

The eight-hour drive stretched into eleven hours. The rental truck overheated twice and Ron had to pull it off the highway. Michael and Ron walked along the interstate somewhere south of Albany, and flagged down a car for a drive to a service station.

"I really appreciate this," Michael told the elderly man who graciously gave him a lift.

"So you're really moving to the North Country?" the driver asked.

"Sure am. Me and my family," Michael said with pride.

"It's certainly God's country, though it does become wicked cold up there. Me and the wife, we like a bit more comfort at our age, and so we settled for a lot less snow. We recently moved south."

After picking up an extra supply of water, potato chips, and cupcakes, a service station mechanic drove both Michael and Ron back to the vehicles. Unfortunately, at this point, everyone was cranky, uncomfortable, and on the verge of exhaustion. Michael rallied and broke up the tension with jokes and small bits of humor.

Late that night, the caravan finally pulled into the driveway on Beaver Ridge. Michael carried the children up to bed—any room was sufficient for the first night. He figured the girls would check out the house in the morning and pick out whichever bedroom suited them. They all would need time to investigate this large home.

"Let's just carry in what we need for the morning," Michael said. "We'll unpack the truck tomorrow when we're not so tired."

"The only essential thing tonight is my shotgun," Ron said. "That little baby will snuggle up real close to my body tonight. What with this ferocious wilderness around, you don't know if there is a bear around, or a wolf, or some strange beast looking to ravage my body."

After a cup of hot tea, the three adults located a sofa and an empty bed, and everyone fell fast asleep. No one bothered to wash up or undress.

When the sun rose, coffee was already poured into cups, and doughnuts lay temptingly available on a platter. Cammi had dragged herself up before anyone had awakened. Though she had collapsed the night before with her legs stiff and her back aching, she was ready to supervise the unloading of the rental truck.

After everyone took a steaming hot shower, they all pitched in to rearrange the furniture left in place by the previous owners. Then they incorporated their transported belongings into the house. It was a strenuous long day, and the girls went to bed early exhausted from the excitement.

The weary threesome sat around the table later that night sharing a quickly prepared tuna casserole. After a couple of beers and two bottles of wine to celebrate their accomplishments, they sat up late into the night talking. Ron surprised Michael and Cammi when he told them that he would love to retire to the country one day. He promised he would return to see them and bring Marie and the boys. Maybe they would scout around for a small place of their own, he had said.

"You suppose maybe we could be neighbors again?" Ron asked with a grin. He felt uncomfortable about having to say good-bye to his friends. He knew it would be awhile before he would see Mike and Cammi again, and he would miss the bond they had formed.

"The solitude sure does grow on you," Ron admitted.

"The crispness in the air certainly makes you more tolerable," Cammi kidded.

Michael and Cammi walked Ron outside. They talked for a long time, thanking him over and over for his help and support.

"We couldn't have done this without your help," said Michael, shaking Ron's hand.

"I hope to see you again. Next visit bring along Marie, and we'll show you both a good time. Of course, now that you know where we live, we probably won't be able to get rid of you guys."

Ron made a promise to visit them soon, and Cammi surprised herself by crying. The rental truck sputtered and clanked as Ron pulled out of the long steep driveway. They waved until he was completely out of sight.

On Ron's next trip to the Adirondack Mountains, Marie and the boys accompanied him. They never visited the Fanelli family in the rental home though. Instead, their next visit two years later was in Michael and Cammi's newly purchased house on the Old Mill Road.

During the following years, the friends exchanged intermittent phone conversations full of laughter and information, and they exchanged Christmas cards, each one filled with a chatty note outlining their present life experiences.

The Fanelli family had no idea that they had reached the edge, tottering between reality and dreams.

# BENNY TREADWELL
# FLOYD'S BIRTHDAY

▼

"Eleven years old. That's almost how old I was when you first came here to live. You keep growing this fast and you'll soon pass me by, Cuz."

Benny presented Floyd with a special gift wrapped neatly in the *Adirondack Daily Enterprise* newspaper and tied with hay bale cord.

Floyd ripped open the present revealing a beautifully hand carved model of an Adirondack boat. The name, *Floyd M. Will*, and his birth date was carved into the bottom of the wooden boat.

"Did you carve this yourself?"

Floyd's expression revealed complete delight in the special gift. Benny knew that only Floyd could express such unabashed happiness and joy. He had not changed his demeanor of simple innocence since the day he arrived to live with them.

"Yes, I did Cuz, just for you. I thought you would like to have this model of the boat we use on our adventures together."

Benny whispered in his ear. "I have some other adventures planned and some more cigars we can enjoy when we're finally alone."

"No more surprises like last winter, I hope."

"What did Benny give you for your birthday?" Aunt Geraldine came around the corner of the house carrying a plate of sweet cakes she had baked for her only son on his special day.

"Look, Ma, he carved it himself." Floyd proudly showed off his newest treasure.

"How nice of you to make that, Benny." She smiled, but her insincerity was obvious, and so was her constant forced attempt to show pleasure in anything Benny did. She was especially vocal when Benny got Floyd into trouble, and Uncle Benjamin punished Floyd. She was waiting for the day the Treadwell's would discover that their son was the troublemaker in the family, not Floyd.

"Did you show Benny the gift I gave you?"

"No, not yet." Floyd proudly held up his arm displaying a silver bracelet with the image of a bear engraved on it.

"Looks swell," Benny said, but he was really thinking it was a silly gift to give an eleven year old.

"You remember to take it off and put it safely in your pocket if you decide to go tearing into the woods climbing on trees and rocks. You're bound to lose it that way, and then you'll want me to go buy you another to replace it."

"Yes, Ma."

"You know he always behaves as you wish, Aunt Geraldine," Benny said in defense of his pal.

To avoid a confrontation, Aunt Geraldine turned on her heels, her taffeta undergarments rustling. The boys heard a "Humph!" escape her lips as she stomped away.

"My mother gets upset with you all the time," Floyd said. "It's really not fair to you. I don't know why she keeps doing that."

"It's really all right Floyd; don't worry a hoot about it. I think she lost her patience exactly like my grandma did when she got old. My very own grandma used to think I was a bad kid too."

"I know you're not."

Floyd hugged Benny around the waist and then quickly pulled away in embarrassment. Benny tousled Floyd's hair noticing how short and fragile the boy still was.

"You are my favorite friend too," Benny said. "Happy Birthday, Floyd."

Floyd gazed at his cousin in adoration.

Just then, Joe called out from the open door of the barn; he was carrying a heavy bucket full of water.

Floyd waved at Joe and he and Benny sauntered over to speak with him.

"What do you fellas' got planned for today?" Joe asked.

"Aunt Geraldine is packing a lunch for us. We gotta' check on two job sites for my father, and then we plan to go to Upper St. Regis. But first, we'll probably stop off at the Ennis camp and visit their daughter for a spell." Benny had a mischievous gleam in his eyes and a naughty curve to his crooked smile.

"Why not come along."

"Sorry, I have to accompany my father to the doctor. I'm sure that's going to be a boring long day. He's not feeling so good, and I have to drive the team for him." Joe had developed into a capable driver and was rapidly becoming an experienced horseman.

"You know, I'd much rather spend the day with you fellas' charming little Miz Ennis right out of her bloomers." Joe smiled.

"Well, I think it best you care for your father and leave the charming to real men," Benny said laughing.

"Come boys," Aunt Geraldine called. "Got your lunch packed, Floyd. Joe, you traveling the day with these boys?"

"No, ma'am. I promised to drive my father into town."

She walked over to Floyd carrying a basket brimming with goodies. Joe caught a whiff of the delicious aroma of fresh baked bread and swooned.

Noticing this Aunt Geraldine said, "We have plenty to share, Joe." She opened the basket to reveal a loaf of warm fresh bread and some cold fried chicken, sweet cakes and fruit. Joe was not the least bit shy about pulling apart the loaf and stuffing a huge chunk of bread in his mouth.

"Um, do you suppose, ma'am that I could also have some of those sweet cakes?"

Aunt Geraldine was generous in sharing the food she had prepared. Her main objective was to pack some meat on her son's skinny bones.

The boys sat together as Joe devoured every bit of his food.

"Let's go, Cuz, before it gets too late in the day," Benny finally said.

"Don't go getting that boy into trouble on his birthday," Joe called out to them as they headed down the road toward the lake, carrying the lunch basket between them.

Aunt Geraldine was out front when the boys passed the house.

"I'll fix you a special birthday supper, Floyd. Benny don't you go and keep him out too late!"

She waved a brisk good-bye, and then reached to pick up the Persian carpet she had just shaken the dust from, and carried it into the house.

"Looks like my father left us his favorite boat to use today," Benny said when they reached the dock.

"He doesn't usually leave this one for us, claims the engine is too powerful for me to maneuver around the lake."

"Maybe he left it especially for us to use on my birthday," Floyd said.

Benny smiled and shrugged his shoulders.

They spent a wonderful afternoon together. They inspected a lumber delivery on one job site and the progress of another. The second site comprised of four outbuildings, a bowling alley, and a boathouse. They stopped off to visit with Susan Ennis, but were disappointed to discover that she and her mother were visiting family in Vermont.

After completion of their schedule for the day, the two boys relaxed on dock, their feet dangling in the water. Floyd splashed Benny and a cold stream of water hit him square in the face.

Benny remained calm. "Funny, very funny," he said, and wiped his face with his shirttail.

Floyd giggled and reached for the lunch basket. He grabbed, and ate the last sweet cake. "Mmmmmmmm, my mother sure knows how to bake," he managed to say, his cheeks bulging, and crumbs spilling out of his mouth.

"Didn't she ever teach you any manners?"

Still full from lunch, the boys lay on their backs on the splintered wood watching the clouds move swiftly overhead. The sun felt pleasantly warm on their faces. Loons floated quietly over the calm water, occasionally dipping their heads beneath the surface.

"Oops, almost forgot something important." Benny jumped up and ran to the boat. He carried back with him a small canvas bag.

"Now, how about a Cuban smoke?" He held out a long cigar. Floyd took the cigar, bit off the tip, and spit it into the water.

"My, my, just like the big boys do," Benny said, as Floyd lit the cigar and puffed bonfire-size circles of smoke around his head.

"How far is Cuba from here?" Floyd asked wistfully.

"Pretty far south. Where did you hear about it except in the cigars that we smoke?"

"I learned in school that President Teddy Roosevelt went to a place called San Juan Hill to fight with the Rough Riders," Floyd said.

"He's not our president anymore."

"If he isn't, who is?"

"I'm not sure, but I know for a fact that Teddy Roosevelt is not our president any more. Bet you didn't know that he was up here hiking on Marcy when someone delivered the message that he was suddenly a president," Benny said.

"You telling me another story?" Floyd asked.

"No, really! He spent a lot of time here in these mountains, hunting, and fishing, and I heard tell that Paul Smith knows him personally." Benny said.

Floyd wasn't sure he believed a word of this and was mulling over the information when Benny pulled a photo from his pocket.

"Want to see a naked lady?" Benny said teasingly, hiding the photo from view.

"You really have picture of a naked lady?"

Floyd struggled to pry open Benny's grasp on the picture, but failed.

"I'll let you look if you sit still."

Benny displayed a picture of a woman with huge bare breasts and nipples, her hair piled high on her head. Her right hand cupped the right breast, and she had an alluring expression on her face.

"Is that what they look like?" Floyd asked, while tracing the outline of her nipple with his finger.

"I never thought bosoms looked like that." The cigar was precariously resting between his two small fingers.

"What did you suppose they looked like any way?" Benny asked.

"I don't really know. I never thought much about it before now."

Benny slapped Floyd squarely in the middle of his back sending him lurching forward.

"Now I know for sure your fibbing." He paused to take notice of the sun.

"We better get a move on, the sun will be setting soon, and your mother will wup my bare arse if I don't get you home for supper in time. Especially today being her baby boy's eleventh birthday."

They loaded the lunch basket onto the boat, and with the cigars clenched between their teeth they untied and pushed off the dock.

"Good thing we have the boat with the more powerful gas engine, now we can get home quicker." Benny said.

"Can I sit on the bow with my feet in the water?" Floyd begged.

"I hate when you do that."

"I'll be careful and hold on tight, I promise. Come on, don't forget it *is* my birthday."

"I give up," Benny said. He accelerated and moved the boat into the open lake out of view of the dock. Floyd was happy positioned on the bow, straddling both sides, the cool water rushing past his toes.

"Will you take me to Cuba when we both get bigger?" Floyd called out over his shoulder.

"Why would you want to go to Cuba?"

"I want to see the place where Teddy was. The battle of San Juan Hill sounded exciting when I heard about it."

"Yeah, I'll take you, just as long as you don't keep on being a troublemaker."

The boat glided across the top of the water at optimum speed. For one short instant, the bright sunlight blinded Benny. He heard Floyd scream, "Look out!"

There was a thunderous grinding noise under the boat; suddenly the hull was airborne. Benny felt himself catapulted from the rear of the boat and into the water. In a split second of pure panic, he found himself struggling underwater. He surfaced and glimpsed the damaged boat slowly sinking a distance away, and Floyd was nowhere in sight.

# THE AFTERMATH

▼

Five hours later, Benny vaguely recognized the sound of a gasoline engine in the far distance. Suddenly alert, he thought he glimpsed tiny lights from multiple search vessels advancing toward him.

"Benny, Floyd! Benny, Floyd!" disembodied voices called out.

Benny coughed and tried to summon the strength to speak."Over here! This direction. Over this way," he cried weakly.

With all the energy depleted from his body, he struggled to wave his hand, but could not. His arms felt too heavy and limp. His clothes were clammy and he was freezing, and his teeth were chattering unmercifully. More lights became visible, and they turned in the proximity of his direction, and then picked up speed. He heard voices call out in the blackness.

"We found them, follow me! This way!"

The tiny boat lights grew larger until a boulder barely jutting above the water-line was illuminated. Among all the dark and indistinguishable faces in the boat, Benjamin's panic-stricken face appeared out of the night. "Thank the Lord, we've found them."

From the darkness, Benjamin leaped onto the boulder. The lantern he held shone a bright light onto Benny's face, which revealed a stunned expression. Floyd's broken body, with a huge bloodied gash on his forehead, lay across Benny's lap. Benjamin knelt beside the boys. He was horrified at the expression on Floyd's face; his eyes open, and staring forever into the black moonless night.

"Oh no! Is he dead?" There was disbelief in his father's trembling voice. "Benny what happened?"

His father gently slid Floyd's body away from Benny and into his own arms.

Benny shook his head, seemingly incoherent and unaware of his surroundings.

"My God! Come here, boys. Benny is fine, but we lost Floyd. The dear child is dead."

A commotion ensued among the men as they passed along the information, then cries of *Damn!* and, *Oh my God!* Some of the men began to cry and others voiced an anguished distress over the sight of the small dead boy.

"Damn, and it was his birthday today!" said one man.

Benny started to cry and reached for his father.

"He died when we hit something," sobbed Benny. "Something hit the bottom of the boat and tore it apart."

"Did you see what it was?" asked another man.

Benny grabbed at Floyd and shook his limp arm.

"Floyd you saw it! You screamed. Floyd what did we hit? There was a monster under the boat, right? It tore into us, I didn't see it coming," Benny said hysterically.

Hands from the men appeared out of the darkness, and gently lifted the dead boy's body. From another direction, a man grabbed a tarp, another covered Benny with a woolen blanket, and another one helped Benny's father into the boat.

The excitement and the noises drowned out Benny's shocked response. "I didn't see it, Floyd saw it coming. It was a monster hiding under the boat!"

When they reached shore, Benny shoved his hands deep into his pockets to keep from trembling. To his amazement, he felt Floyd's silver bracelet still lying inside his pocket where Floyd had placed it earlier in the day for safekeeping.

Shadowy forms delivered a long flatbed wagon to the shoreline, and two men gently placed the body on the wagon bed. Benny jumped in to sit beside the bundled tarp, and they began the solemn trek home where Aunt Geraldine awaited news of her son.

As the wagon, burdened with the weight of its gruesome cargo, rounded the curve of the Old Mill Road, the house came into view. Dreading to face Aunt Geraldine, Benny got up on his knees as the wagon drew ever closer to its destination. The house stood ablaze with every light shining, sending rays of incandescent beams out the windows in every direction. Delusional, he imagined it resembled a lighthouse perched atop a tall hill above the ocean beckoning ships to safety. He realized he had never viewed his house this way, and the sight of it caused him to tremble in fear and trepidation.

The first inkling that the wagon was returning prompted frantic movement and activity among the crowd standing on the porch praying for a glimpse of the return of the rescue crew. Benny recognized the shapes of two women lifting their long skirts running down the steps toward the returning wagon.

Even in the darkness, without full recognition, he knew the shapes running toward him were that of his mother and his aunt Geraldine. They were screaming the names of their beloved sons, and frantically waving their hands in the air as they ran. Crowds of people began pouring out of the house and into the road; some screaming, others praying.

A hysterical swarm of humanity reached the wagon all at once. Benny's mother clawed at his arm. He felt frightened by the agitated commotion that surrounded the wagon. Unseen hands pulled aside the tarp revealing the identity of the body. An interminable split second of shocked silence was followed by agonizing screams of grief.

Somehow, Aunt Geraldine leaped onto the flatbed with such force that it unsteadied, and she tried to no avail to awaken the pale corpse that was once her son. The men struggled in an attempt to restrain her. Eventually they subdued her, but she fought them with such ferocity that finally four men were obliged to carry her toward the house. Half carrying and half dragging her, Aunt Geraldine's wild eyes locked onto Benny's face.

"Why wasn't it you instead of him!" she screamed. "It should have been you!"

The rest of the night was a blur for Benny. He remembered being wrapped in blankets and placed in front of a blazing fire. His mother piled on the blankets in an attempt to calm the convulsions that overtook his weakened body. His sister Catherine sat next to him, her little arms cradled his head.

"Where is Floyd now?" he asked through chattering teeth.

His mother pulled a chair close to him and sat down.

"They are in the parlor behind the playroom preparing his body for burial," she answered in a hushed tone.

"Why did it have to happen?"

"It was an accident."

"No. Something ripped the bottom of the boat apart."

"What Benny, what was it?"

"I couldn't see anything, it all happened so fast."

"Maybe you hit a rock."

"No, I know I didn't. There was something huge in the water, the sun blinded me, so I didn't see it, but Floyd did."

"Rest, my darling. I am so happy you are home safe. It could have been that both of you were killed. God has truly spared us some small amount of agony."

After he was helped to his room, his sister came in dressed in her nightshirt. Catherine latched the door from the inside and pulled a chair close to his bed.

"I'll sit with you tonight. That insane woman will not get in here to hurt you, I promise."

Benny was aware that Catherine sat all night as a sentinel, protecting him from the wrath of Aunt Geraldine.

Tossing, and unable to sleep, he could hear Aunt Geraldine's incessant wailing, her voice hoarse and guttural. "It should have been him!"

Her anguish turned into a prayer of retribution, tormented emotions completely out of control. "God should have made him die instead of you!"

She screamed loud enough for each word spoken to fill the voids in every space, in every stud, beam, and floorboard, in every room from attic to basement. The hate reverberated through the metal ceilings and the grates. She continued throughout the night, with no mercy for the rest of the inhabitants of the house.

Benny lay in bed with his eyes staring at the ceiling. Catherine had dozed off; her hands covered her ears, her head hung lopsided on one shoulder. Sounds from the crazed woman downstairs rang off in the distance as Benny replayed over and over in his mind every miniscule split second. He reenacted every noise and sound up to the precise instant of the destruction of the boat. He reckoned he had made a bad move, one miscalculation that sent Floyd flying off the boat into eternity.

At dawn's light, Benny finally began to cry. Catherine awoke with a start and silently lay down on top of the covers beside him, both sobbing until they were exhausted.

Aunt Geraldine had questions too, but after that first horror-filled night, she appeared to recover from the insane ravings caused by her suffering.

On the second day, she ventured into the kitchen for only a moment to have a cup of hot tea. She then quickly returned to the parlor bolting the door behind her. There she remained vigilant inside the small room alone beside her son's body. They had laid Floyd on a slab of wood covered with a black velvet cloth. He was dressed in the same white shirt he had arrived in more than two years before. The birthday gift she had given him was not found on his body, and she resigned herself that it was most likely lying on the muddy bottom of the lake.

After the burial in the church graveyard, she was not seen during daylight hours, but was secluded inside her quarters immersed in the memories she chose fervently to cling to.

The evening after the burial, Benny sat alone on the front porch. It seemed eons ago that he had so proudly completed its construction. His father came outside to sit with him, and gently laid his hand on Benny's shoulder.

"Why did Floyd have to die?" Benny asked.

"I don't think I can ever answer that question for you, son."

"I can't understand what destroyed the boat. I don't remember any rocks protruding over the waterline. I saw nothing." His lip started to quiver. "I cannot stop thinking about it, I will always try to understand and question *why*."

Father and son spoke for a long time, but there were no answers to the questions raised.

Afterward, during the dead of night, Aunt Geraldine became a nocturnal vision roaming through the yard. Strolling aimlessly among the garden vegetables awaiting harvest, she would slowly find her way to the rear stone steps that led into the forest. To those who saw her, she became a living apparition seemingly gliding over the nightly mists. She never addressed her hateful feelings. She kept locked within her soul extreme hostility, and she prayed each night by candlelight for malevolent retribution.

The Recovery

*March 7, 1917*

*Dearest Catherine,*

*I am sorry I left before you arrived back from your trip to visit your friend Minnie in Plattsburgh. I could not postpone my escape any longer. The house was morbidly silent in your absence and I thought I would lose my mind. What with our mother and father being so damned civil to one another it has been an effort to get through each day, and not forgetting that Aunt Geraldine is forever silent and hateful. I did not realize it was your smiling face and caring love that had kept me here until now. So I packed up and left.*

*Of course, I will miss Joe and his unwavering support and friendship. Only the two of you have provided me with the will to go on, the will to continue to exist. Just last night Father announced that Lenny, Joe's father, has finally been promoted to head foreman, and he put Joe in charge of the logging camp. So I know he will be* leaving soon to take over his new position. I noticed as of late that Father is finding it more and more difficult to continue to work as hard as he once did. Mother, of course, is no help in that situation. She finally got out of bed and got dressed last week. She made an unexpected trip to the mill, I think to spy on the workers and be sure they are running things up to snuff.

I plan to do some trapping and guide some city folks down in the Glens Falls area. Then I think it's onto New York City. Always wanted to see the Stature of Liberty and find out for myself if this city is worth all the excitement I hear tell. Right now, I am missing you.

Love from your brother, Benny


April 21, 1917

Dearest Brother,

I was shocked beyond description to see your empty room after I arrived home. Unbelievably Mother cried when she told me you had gone. Funny, she never appears that she would miss us while we are here. I noticed Father has been drinking heavy again. We cannot keep enough whiskey in this house. Sometimes he actually becomes abusive, screaming unmercifully at Mother and Aunt Geraldine. Last week he called Aunt Geraldine a lunatic and threatened to send her to the crazy hospital. That provoked her to screaming and crying, running off into the forest. She did not come back for several hours, and the mood here appeared to pass. That crazy woman started baking again since you've been gone from the house. I think she believed that if she baked something you liked it would provide you with pleasure. And God knows that's the last thing she would ever want to do.

I had to store away some linen in the back room and happened to pass Floyd's bedroom. It shocked me to see Mrs. Crazy had his clothes lying out across the bed as if he would arrive home soon and change into them. The room reeked of candle wax. It appears she is battier than we thought. I must admit it brought tears to my eyes to see those clothes again, I so miss the poor boy.

Minnie sends her regards. She has a soft heart for you. I do think that if you asked, she would accept any proposals you would suggest.

The crew in the back quarters asked me about how you are doing. They said they saved you a chair so when you come home you can sit in on their poker games. They *also asked me to remind you that you owe them a bundle of money they have spotted you all these years.*

*It is almost midnight and I just went to close my bedroom window and saw Mrs. Crazy walking out back by the stone steps. That old bat is wearing her nightgown out there, what with the temperature still below freezing. She is not unlike an apparition with the misty fog hanging lightly over the ground she is a living ghost. All the men in the crew have made jokes and bawdy references to her nightly walks in the forest. I see them watch her from the quarter's window. We don't know where she goes, but no one seems to much care anymore.*

*Well, I pray we soon get spring weather. And, I pray for you Brother, and your safe and speedy return home.*

*Love,*
*your sister, Catherine*

*July 15, 1917*

*Dear Son,*

*I have heard rumor from Joe that you are thinking of enlisting in the service of our dear country. The thought of you sent off to war is too gloomy to contemplate. I have fervently prayed for an end to this abominable war, and now I have more reason to wish it would command a definitive peace in the world. So many of your classmates and neighbors have fought valiantly, and buried in our cemetery, lay a few of the unfortunate souls.*

*On the Fourth of July, we had a garden party and invited all the neighbors, some relatives, and business associates. We put out a fine spread—corn on the cob, potato salad, and fresh vegetables of every variety. We churned ice cream until our arms dropped. Your father took it upon himself to decorate the front yard in red, white, and blue bunting, and we had many flags displayed on the lawn. The crew came over after the guests left and devoured everything they saw fit to eat. At dusk, the bats came out of their place in the eves, swooped down on our heads, and chased us all inside.*

*Your sister has been melancholy as of late. I believe the poor girl misses you. Father has gone back to work a bit more earnestly, and has had an architect working on plans for a home to be built in the Lake Clear area. I only go to the mill a day a week now, as Lydia and her husband have been doing a fair job of running things. At least whenever I go there it appears that way, but since it is profitable and earnings are up,*

*I will allow them to take charge of the business. Besides, the doctor says I cannot work as often as I used to any longer.*

*Keep safe, I will continue to pray for peace in the world.*
*Your Mother*


*February 13, 1919*

*Dearest Catherine,*

*Well, I suppose our dear mother's prayers have brought a speedy peace in the world. Being PVT 33 Co 153 Depot Brigade in these last months of the world conflict, I was lucky enough to avoid seeing battle. I am contemplating joining company with the Army Corps of Engineers as soon as possible. But my company consists of some really serious poker players, and by the time my tour is over and I come home, I am going to beat the pants off the crew. How are Lenny and Joe? Is my old tree fort still standing after the arduous winter you have had to endure up there?*

*That is not really why I am writing to you. Your last letter mentions this William fella'. Who is he and what does he mean to you? You mentioned he stays over on Easy Street. How long ago did he move there from Malone? Funny that you mention his house is not far from the original cabin where Grandma once lived fifty-five years ago, when father was little. It makes me uneasy being so far away from you and not able to meet this fella' in person. Is he aware you have a brother in the army? Hope he is intimidated by that and watches his manners.*

*Have to admit, I am beginning to miss home.*

*Love, Benny*


*March 22, 1919*

*Dearest Brother,*

*Your concern tugs at my heartstrings. I will introduce you to William via this post. His father is John Morgan Tyler, and he had been part of an established law practice for many years in Malone. From what William had told me, there was a falling out among the partners and John decided to relocate his practice to Saranac Lake or Lake Placid, which is in dire need of a new law firm. They moved here to set up an office. William just completed his studies and plans to join his father in this endeavor.*

*We met very innocently at church services, and then he stopped at the house to meet with Father to talk about the construction of his new office. Of course, Mrs. Crazy lost her marbles over him. She thinks he is so proper and fancy. Mother distanced herself from the whole affair, she could not care one way or another. Father agrees with me that he is made from solid cloth, a fine upstanding character. I just hate the fact that whenever he visits, Mrs. Crazy has to concoct something really scrumptious and special; luring him into appreciating her more than our own mother or father.*

*I told William about Floyd last night. He was baffled by the circumstances surrounding the cause of the accident. I am glad you and I have been able to speak honestly to one another about that day. Nobody in this house ever mentions Floyd at all, which pains me. I think everyone is afraid Mrs. Crazy will fall off her cliff again. I do not think but for one time that Mother and Mrs. Crazy discussed the accident. However, it was, I believe an uncomfortable situation for Mother. I hate that everyone around this house carries on as though Floyd never existed. Seems to make a mockery of what a fine boy he was.*

*Well, Brother, tell me what you think about William. I know you will not be at a loss of words telling your little sister what you think about a fella' coming around the house to visit. Joe sends his regards and says he wishes you both could hole up in the barn with some beer and talk nonsense into the early morning hours.*

*Your sister who loves you, Catherine*


*December 2, 1919*

*Dear Father,*

*I want to wish all of you a happy and healthy holiday season. I have thirty days leave ahead, but I plan to make a trip to Cuba instead of coming home. I've always wanted to see the famous harbor there and San Juan Hill. It is a place spoken with such reverence I thought to go there and poke around to see what it's all about.*

*Give Mother a kiss for me, and let Catherine know about my plans. I will write again after my return.*

*Love, Benny*

*January 10, 1919*

*Dear Catherine,*

*I had long ago promised Floyd a trip to San Juan Hill, and I have fulfilled the promise. I brought a little bit from him along with me and buried it under a tree in this hallowed ground. It pained me to part with his birthday bracelet and see the last gleam from it disappear under the soil. But somehow, it made me feel better, and I was at once relieved of a small piece of the agonizing guilt I have carried with me since that day.*

*I spent the Christmas holidays there among some happy people. There was much singing and festivities. Far different from the gloomy Christmas you described to me, spent at home. Complete strangers invited me into their home where I spent a few days sharing their happiness, learning their customs, and attempting to speak the language. The food was delicious, and I left there feeling heavier than when I first arrived. It was well worth the long trip, a pilgrimage I had to endure for a small amount of peace.*

*Let William know that I will meet him one day. Somehow, I get the feeling he will still be hanging around the Treadwell residence when I come home.*

*Love, your brother*

*January 15, 1920*

*Dear Ben,*

*Sorry I could not write sooner. William and I have joined ranks with the Winter Carnival Committee and have been busy lately. We are helping in the construction of the ice tower and plan to ski a short race on Mount Pisgah. Of course, I have to make a go of the ice skating contest also. Remember how much faster than you I could skate? If I could beat you, I can win the race! Oh, those childhood rivalries.*

*Just wanted to affirm that I am happy you were able to make your long ago promise to Floyd good. That pilgrimage should ease some of your pain, and I agree the bracelet belongs there, buried among memories of the men that perished on that consecrated ground. I am proud you are my brother and truly love you with all my heart.*

*I hope you come home soon. You will be surprised how Father has aged. He needs to wear a hat now, all the time, to keep his head warm. The little hair he has left now no longer provides him with such warmth. I am working in place of Mother at the mill office keeping the books. It makes her feel better that I am there representing the family, you know how uncomfortable she felt knowing the business was out of her control.*

*William thought us childish and cruel to refer to Mrs. Crazy as such, but he has changed his mind now after watching her nightly journeys into the forest half dressed and seeing how reclusive she is.*

*Love, your sister*

*September 17, 1920*

*Dear Catherine,*

*I am planning to come home spring of next year. I have had it too comfortable these last years by not experiencing the icy, freezing Adirondack winters. But, alas I think it's time. I will be released from the army in early spring. Time off for good behavior, I guess. It has been advantageous to my future earnings in all the education I have gleaned from my tour.*

*I do hope you are able to postpone until springtime your planned marriage with William. You could not proceed prior to my arrival since hopefully; I still rate as the most important man in your life. I will concede to him after our initial meeting and my subsequent approval. I know right now you're smiling fully and understanding that your brother is still bossy and overbearing.*

*And he loves you! How can I ever forget your sincerity in guarding me from that crazed lunatic woman years ago? That took courage! You have quietly stood by me in the background during our early years, and I have learned to appreciate that from you. Of course, that must mean that I have matured. Perish that thought girl, I only humor you as the one person who will be excited when I pull up into the driveway. By the way, how does William cope with a liberated woman fiancée?*

*Give our parents my best. I admit I had hoped to hear from them more often, but some things never change.*

*Love, Benny*

April 24, 1921

*Dear Father,*

*I was shocked to hear that mother has suffered a stroke. The wire I received alluded that she was faring well and on the road to recovery. I plan to be near a telephone line so I will phone as soon as I reach my destination. Please give Mother my most sincere love and affection, along with my prayers for a quick recovery. Catherine has written that the jobs are going well and the crew is now on target with the construction work.*

*I hope that her beau, William is of good nature, and in good steed with the family. He sounds as though he is a likeable chap, but that information comes from Catherine and may be a bit lopsided. Let Lenny and Joe know I will be home soon, hopefully to stay. That depends of course, if I still have a job working with you and the men from the crew.*

*I plan to leave here in the next week and begin my long trek home. Thought you might want to know, I arranged to stop off in Albany to visit some friends for a short while. With my poker earnings, I purchased a Model T Ford Roadster. It has a four-cylinder cycle engine that boasts a twenty-two horsepower motor. With front wheel drive, I do not imagine it will maneuver well, considering the heavy snow we get, but I'll worry about that when winter arrives. The gasoline engine has some powerful potential and I can get this baby upward of thirty miles an hour. Think about that! I will be happy to take you for an outing to show off my new toy.*

*Love, your son Benny*

# BENNY TREADWELL
# THE HOMECOMING

▼

Benny had twenty more miles to go before his long awaited arrival home. A knot had formed in his stomach making him slightly nauseous. He could not determine if the queasy feeling was from driving on the bumpy roads or from the anticipation of going home after four long years. When he turned onto the Old Mill Road, the familiarity of the surroundings brought a chill to his spine. The pines and the musty smell of the primeval forest brought back a flood of memories. The whole experience of coming home was surprisingly unnerving. He remembered by heart the last bend in the road, where the house would finally come into view.

There was nothing welcoming about his home. The afternoon light reflected from the windows and made the house look gloomy and dark. The first glimpse of the place terrified him, and filled him with panic. He took several deep breaths to calm himself.

What the hell is going on with me? Without any forewarning, bile rose in his throat. Everyone must be waiting for me, watching from behind the windows.

As his car approached the driveway, a sudden rush of people came from the house. Some ran down the front steps to greet him in the street. He began to perspire. This sight reminded him of that ill-fated night seven years before when they brought Floyd's body home.

The first person to reach the car was Catherine. Benny pulled the hand brake and she jumped into the front seat beside him. His sister had matured into a beautiful woman. She threw her arms around him and kissed his face. Her long brown hair glistened red highlights in the sunshine, and he noticed a hint of makeup on her cheeks.

His father swung open the driver's door, and Benny stepped out of the car.

"Benny, I can't believe you're really here," his eyes glistened as he stood back and admired his son. "It's been four years. You look great, son," he said as the two embraced.

Benny glanced over his shoulder and saw his mother standing on the front steps. She was leaning on a cane appearing quite sickly. Benny rushed to greet her.

"I missed you so, son," she said. "There has been a large void in this house since you've been gone."

As Benny hugged his mother, he could feel the bones up and down her spine betraying how frail she had become. He stood back disbelieving that this gray haired woman, her face lined with deep trenches, was really the woman he called Mother. The last four years had taken a toll.

He noticed Aunt Geraldine on the front porch carefully maneuvering an obviously heavy punch bowl filled with a light brown liquid swirling over ice. Glasses stood on a table and a tray of fresh baked cookies lay nearby. He was astonished that his aunt would have involved herself in the preparations for his arrival.

Benny also noticed a young handsome man leaning against the cedar tree in the front yard. Benny walked directly over to him and reached to shake his hand. "And you must be William."

William smiled. "Yes, I am."

Benny noticed William's unassuming manner, liked him immediately, and appreciated him even more when he saw William steal a glance in Catherine's direction and wink. She reciprocated, her face radiant.

"I am glad you put off the wedding so I could join in the festivities."

"Would not have had it any other way," William said.

Suddenly a group of men from the crew appeared. Joe grabbed Benny from behind in a body hug and lifted him off his feet.

"Damn, it's good to see you. Where the hell did those muscles come from?" he asked, punching Benny on the upper arm.

"All those pushups I was required to do in the service got my wimpy ass in shape, boy!"

Joe had grown larger and appeared to be more muscular than Benny remembered. He had turned twenty-two his last birthday.

The whole party moved toward the porch. Suddenly Benny was face to face with his aunt Geraldine. She had gained weight. Her face was sallow and puffy accentuating the dark circles under her eyes. Her straight hair drawn into a tight bun did nothing to soften the fiery hatred that still flared in her eyes.

"Happy you're back," she said indifferently, then promptly turned and disappeared into the house. Benny saw the lie in the squint and glare of her eyes. Without further ado, everyone attacked the cookie tray and poured punch into the small punch glasses.

"If you want something a little more potent, see me in the barn tonight," Joe whispered, his hand covering his mouth.

Benny smiled. "You don't have to ask me more than once."

After a delicious dinner of Benny's favorite, pork roast with apple stuffing and boiled potatoes, everyone enjoyed fresh vanilla ice cream with raspberry preserves. Benny finally relaxed, but not before sharing several glasses of whiskey with his father.

"Strange, that in spite of the way Aunt Geraldine hates me she would prepare my favorite meal."

"I admit that I had to speak with her last week," his father began as the two of them sat outside on the porch swing. "I told her in no uncertain terms that if she could not control her emotions she would have to leave before your arrival. I know she visits the cemetery every week, and I was sure she would stay on with Floyd buried so close by here."

He took a long puff on his cigar and studied the smoke until it dissipated.

"I explained that life is hard enough without her relentless grudges causing additional friction. She promised she would try just for the sake of continuing to live here. She has been a capable nurse for your mother, so it's important she stay, at least for now."

Pausing, his bottom lip began to quiver.

"I cannot explain to you Benny, but the last years have been most difficult; what with your mother's health declining and all. And we can't forget the tragic mishap on the lake. There were times I thought I could not go on."

He halted in an attempt to recover his composure.

"That's when the business saved me, gave me a small reason to push on. Then when you said you were coming home, I was happy. After all these years I found something substantial to hang onto, felt glad I had not ended it all. It gave me reason to live, just to see you again." He started to cry and buried his head in his hands.

Benny wrapped an arm around his father's shoulders.

"I'm back to stay, work with the crew, and get our business revitalized. After traveling around, I have gathered some new ideas we can incorporate into our construction work." Benny smiled. "You'll see, life will begin to look rosy again."

Catherine and William stepped outside to join them. Father got up and quickly and disappeared into the house.

"So when is the big day?" Benny asked.

"Most likely, we'll arrange a fall wedding. It's so lovely that time of year," Catherine answered.

"I can't wait. I hope you know, William that my sister is a gem. She will be a huge asset to your life. I know she has been an asset to mine."

William smiled contentedly. He appeared relaxed and quite familiar with being a part of the Treadwell household.

"Don't worry; I think you are already aware that I will take excellent care of your sister." He reached over to take hold Catherine's hand.

"I do. I knew the minute I set eyes on you. Look forward to a happy life ahead for all of us." Benny raised his whiskey glass and William reciprocated with a proper Boy Scout salute.

During the early morning hours, Benny heard footsteps downstairs. Aunt Geraldine had completed her supposedly secretive nightly excursion into the forest and was just getting back to her room. Unable to rest, Benny got up from bed and went outside. An early morning mist hung over the grass and there was promise of a sunny, warm day. Benny noticed Joe feeding the horses in the barn.

"Up early. Or did you come out here just to lend me a hand?"

"No, I didn't sleep so well. I heard the old bat coming home to hang her body in the rafters."

Joe laughed. "You must have taken notice of a few changes around here, what with being away some four years."

"Yes, I was surprised though to see my mother in such poor health."

"Don't go worrying about her, she'll outlive us all. It's actually your father who we've been concerned with."

Joe struggled for the right words."He's not been himself in years. Sure as shit, the old cigar is still stuck in his face, but he's changed, gotten into some problems, I think. Couple of months ago, we got a call from out by Tupper Lake that he was so drunk and unruly they'd thrown his ass out of a bar. Had to go rescue him from off the street and cart him home. Have even found him here in the barn in the morning, all laid out flat ass drunk, asleep in the hay."

Benny began to perspire.

Joe appeared uncomfortable and moved closer to Benny."I think it's been a long time coming, a marriage issue. They pretend nothing is going on, but we all know there's a lot of hate between those two. I think it's time I come clean and tell you 'bout something that happened here a couple years back. I wanted you to hear it from me first."

"What about?" Benny asked.

"Well," Joe sat down on a hay bale across from Benny, "About two winters ago, them La Due boys went out on the lake ice fishing. Well, they sat there awhile freezing their tails off when they snagged onto something."

"What was it?"

"It was an old leather saddlebag, the kind you strap onto a motorbike. Inside were some papers with about seven thousand dollars cash money, and they turned it over to the authorities."

He paused. "Well, you know how nosey them two are. They went down in the springtime after the thaw and started snooping around. They were seen feeling around on the lake bottom with their oar and stuff. They even resorted to free diving. Well, it wasn't long before they found themselves a real monster. A motorcycle with a sidecar just hung up solid, with chains all around it holding it tight in place on a rock. That motorcycle was just below the waterline, side car up, all mangled and tore up."

Benny swallowed hard. He focused his eyes on one corner of the barn where a huge spider was busy spinning itself an enormous web.

"Do you think that's the thing I hit?" he finally asked.

"We know that's what your boat hit, because splintered pieces of wood were still embedded in the tore-up carcass of the motorcycle."

"Does Catherine know about this?"

"Yeah. She knows. We both decided it best if you heard 'bout it from me after you got home."

"Who do they think did this?"

"Well, the state police went to perform a real detective investigation. Started shortly after the moneybag was found, and then it got hot and heavy after the bike materialized. It seems the guy who owned the motorcycle has been missing some eight, nine years. He was some fella' from Brasher Falls. They know he didn't just hang his bike up on some boulders in the lake and walk off, so they dredged the lake for information concerning his whereabouts."

"What did they find?"

"Nuttin', but I could have told them that before they went through all that trouble. So, it sounds like nobody knows what really happened. The chain was just an ordinary chain that possibly dislodged and drifted onto the boulder where it hung up tight. The chain was maybe twenty or thirty feet long, and completely wrapped around and around them rocks. There has been all kinds of gossip and rumor, but no real conclusion, because there ain't no rotten body been found." Joe hesitated.

Benny shook his head in an attempt to absorb all this information.

"All the police found out was this guy had ordered lumber milled. He was building a house over in Brasher. Seems he owed your mother seven thousand dollars when he came to town to pay it. Would stand to reason if it was robbery, the money would have vanished along with the body. But the money shows up first, making things look real suspicious. The biggest relief to everyone was that he had never made it to the mill to pay, because he had the cash stashed inside his bags. And, the bill is stilled owed on an open account at the office."

"This would mean he went somewhere else before going to pay his account," Benny surmised.

"That's the way the police see it happening. They had a talk with your mother and father who were able to verify that they hadn't collected payment on the account. Your parents don't remember seeing him except when the order was originally placed. It caused the county, all the way over east to Plattsburgh and parts south to Albany to talk shit. You know gossip is the only thing keeps us alive during the winter months."

"I wish somebody would have told me about this sooner."

"And, what would that have accomplished? You were away in the army, remember? We knew this information would be a lot for you to absorb." Joe stood and picked a rake up off the ground. "We had a discussion. Me, Catherine, and your father. We did what we thought was best for you at the time."

"So, do you think this guy's dead body will ever show up?"

"Don't believe it ever will. Way too many years and way too many fish in that lake."

# THE FANELLI'S NEW HOME

▼

"Gosh baby, you know I've had my heart set on a log cabin home since we moved here. I've been looking around, pricing them."

"Come on Cammi, I saw this place, you'll love it. My buddy Tom from the electric company, drove me by to peek at it yesterday, it's gorgeous! Victorian gingerbread trim around the roof and diamond leaded glass front doors. We stopped off after work and looked in the downstairs windows. There are all kinds of carved trim, and a couple of skylights set into the roof. Tom said he heard the guy who owns it really needs to sell, needs the money or something. He thinks we can buy it dirt cheap."

"Why doesn't Tom buy it if he knows so much about it? I really didn't want to have to renovate an old house. It's so much work. I've finally succeeded in having some precious little time to myself."

"Please honey, come along with me, and just look. Maybe you'll fall in love with it too."

"Well, it won't hurt to go by and check it out. Go ahead and call the guy and set up an appointment." She sighed.

"Well, I already did and we tour the house Sunday afternoon." Michael had a playful grin on his face. "The owner only uses the house as a hunting lodge now, but he used to live in it a long time ago. It's been standing vacant for years. He's planning on coming up with his two sons the first day of deer season on Friday."

"Okay, so it really didn't pay to even argue about it, you should have told me we were going to see the house whether I wanted to or not."

"I'm sorry, honey. It is the kind of house I have always dreamed of owning. An old Victorian home located on acreage in the woods. Can't you just see it? Shit, if you really don't like it, it's okay, but just come by and take a quick look at it."

"Man, I can't fight you. You're relentless! Your sister Lucille told me so years ago."

"But you got to know that to me a log cabin has no character. This place has character with a capital C."

"It might have character, but I hope it has central heating too."

"Well, I did spot an old cast iron stove in the kitchen." Michael laughed jokingly.

"Oh boy! I can't wait to see the headlines. City girl cooks on wood burning stove. Burns family house down to the ground!"

Michael and Cammi stopped by to view the house about 4:30 in the afternoon. The sun hid behind dark forbidding clouds. Icy drizzles of rain peppered the air. Cammi had to admit the house was impressive from the outside. The yellow paint on the clapboard siding brightened an otherwise somber appearance.

"Come in, come in, please." A man wearing only thermal long johns greeted the couple at the front door. A huge roaring fire in the fireplace lent some warmth to the cluttered front living room. Three rifles leaned against the wall in one corner of the room. Wet camouflage clothing and bright orange outerwear lay haphazardly on the floor.

"Call me Calvin," the man said, and ushered them inside.

Cammi felt chills quiver up her spine. She did not know if the chills were from the cold air or from this unsavory looking man. Michael suddenly became acutely aware of how Calvin looked at Cammi when she came into the room. The strange man's eyes caressed her every movement. Michael struggled to squelch the sudden urge to grab one of the rifles and plaster Calvin's brains all over the walls.

"Sit down and relax," Calvin said, his lecherous grin revealed an almost toothless mouth.

Calvin made space on a sagging old sofa by swiping his arm against dirty clothes and empty beer cans. The items plopped unceremoniously onto the paint splattered oak floor. He grinned at Cammi. She watched his piercing eyes scan her body as if she were naked.

"So, you're interested in the house," he started. "Bobby, come in here and escort this fine couple to take a look around our house."

A boy about sixteen came in from the kitchen, his mouth stuffed with a baloney sandwich, mustard stains on his chin. He was a much younger, less worn image of his father except he had teeth that protruded and were too large for his mouth.

After a complete in-depth tour, Cammi felt overwhelmed. There was plenty of work necessary to renovate the spacious home.

"I'll hold the papers and make it as easy as possible for you folks and your family to move in here." Calvin directed the conversation to Michael, since Michael seemed the more interested of the two.

Cammi began to perspire. She felt pressured and overwhelmed.

Calvin noted the glimmer of interest in Michael's eyes and continued the hard sell.

"Me and the boys, we leave here in a couple of weeks, and you can both come back during that time and inspect the place on your own. The next-door neighbor holds a key while we're gone." He turned to Cammi. "You, little lady, sure don't look convinced this is the house for you."

Cammi shrugged, feeling even more apprehensive. Her mind was unconsciously recalling the frightening dream she had before they left for vacation.

"It certainly is big," was all she could think to say.

"Yeah, what I plan to do is move my trailer over to the far edge of the property line. You know, I haven't actually lived inside this place for some thirty years or more. At that time, I moved to Rochester, married, and stayed there. My wife has been up here with me once or twice. She's scared to death to be left here alone. She says she hears stuff, noise, and things, and she claims the place is haunted. But, I tried to explain to her that it's an old house, and all old houses make creaking noises."

Cammi raised her eyebrows and attempted to interrupt the conversation, but Michael immediately stopped her, raising his finger to his lips. He was excited at the prospect of buying a house thought to be haunted.

"Now-a-days, my boys come up here only 'bout a day once a year to go hunting. My wife usually stays behind in Rochester. I can sell it to you real cheap, mate. You can actually steal it from me now the way I feel. Go ahead and make a killing, com'on."

Cammi studied Michael and saw the battle was lost. She knew he had already made up his mind.

"A thousand smackerroos gets you moved in and when I go home, I can have mortgage papers drawn up by my lawyer. Won't even need a visit to a bank or nothin'. You only need to send the payments directly to me every month."

With a shortage of cash a huge issue for the Fanelli family, Michael felt the offer hard to refuse.

The deal was quickly concluded.

"I'm so tired I feel nauseated," Cammi complained as she stuffed wispy strands of curly hair into her old Mets baseball cap. White spackle and several colors of paint dotted the cap.

"Please just make me a quick sandwich," Michael begged as he climbed down from a rickety ladder carrying a large plastic bucket half filled with flat white ceiling paint. "I'll finish the last bit of painting if you can make me a ham and cheese with mayo."

"Gosh, honey, we've been working like maniacs the last few months, and every time we finish one thing on the list, twenty more projects appear. I don't think we'll ever be done renovating this place. My bet is we'll run out of money before we run out of muscle."

"You'll see, baby, it'll be worth the extra effort. At least we have one heating system installed in the living room. And once we actually move in, we'll have completed the most important projects. I mean, just insulating those four outside walls and hanging the new sheetrock will help contain the heat."

She looked at him with an expression of disbelief.

"Do you mean to tell me Michael, that by insulating four walls, this creaky old house is going to stay warm? Why in some rooms the snow will drift in through the openings in the walls."

"No it won't. We're air tight," he moaned.

"And, the windows, won't we lose a bunch of heat through the glass?"

"Well, hopefully I can get some storm windows hung before winter actually sets in."

"I wish we could afford heating the back breakfast room and the pantry in the kitchen area," Cammi sighed.

"Why? Doesn't stoking the old cast iron stove give you a cozy feeling of nostalgia?"

"Nostalgia, my ass. And, Mr. Homeowner, check out my newest jeans." She revealed a pattern of holes where muriatic acid had splattered when she cleaned some old paint from the fireplace bricks.

"Got no time to worry about jeans, honey. It's more important to scrape away some of this old paint before we move in."

"Aren't you afraid the lead in the paint might stunt your growth?" she said, exiting the room to get something for Michael to eat. She felt a hard knot in her stomach. Be it from exhaustion or from dread, something about the house gave her the willies. But she was realistic enough to understand there was no putting off the inevitable move into what she now referred to as "the house that Michael built."

Two weeks later, they had actually finished enough of the planned work to move in with Jenna and Renee.

"Come outside Cammi, I've a surprise for you," Michael yelled into an open window off the porch. He had seen Cammi inside hanging wallpaper.

He had mounted a large wooden sign out by the road. *Michael Fanelli, General Contractor.*

"It looks great, honey," she said proudly. She put her arms around his neck and kissed him.

"This is it, baby. We are going to make a fortune here. You'll see it's only the beginning." He took her in his arms and twirled her around.

One of our neighbors I met down by the lake yesterday, told me that the original owners of this place were building contractors also, and their sign was mounted right about here some fifty some odd years ago. So, I thought I would mount mine in approximately the same spot."

Jenna tugged at Cammi's shirt. "Mom, Mrs. Titus asked me to feed her horse Queenie once a day. She is going to pay me five dollars a week. She said that if I had my own horse she would let me keep it in her empty stall for free. Please, I'll take care of a horse myself and my tenth birthday is coming up next month. Please, please, please!"

Cammi and Michael rolled their eyes.

"You're like your father. You think if you ask me enough times you'll wear me down until I consent. Glad you have the job feeding the Titus horse, but we'll have to talk seriously about buying one of our own."

Jenna pouted, turned away, and stomped into the house. She slammed the front door behind her.

"Sometimes she manages to look and behave just like her dad," Cammi kidded.

"Well, I was thinking it would be fun to get a horse for her. There is not very much for her to do out here in the sticks. It's not exactly like the ballet school is located down the street. The only amusement she has is to ride her bike up and down the road, besides if we live in the country we can learn to live like country folks do."

"You mean country folks all own horses? Be real!"

Cammi had a feeling she was not going to be able to fight the inevitable purchase of a horse for Jenna. She only hoped they weren't going to have to buy one for Renee also. One thing about Renee was that she preferred reading quietly in her bedroom and fiddling with her piano. She did not care much for horses.

When Jenna's birthday arrived, Michael and Cammi purchased a horse for seventy-five dollars. They imagined the horse would be easy to care for. The animal was a stubborn old mare called Lightning. The people they purchased her from had to go out into the woods to fetch her. She was a broad, but smallish horse and difficult to control. Her coat was almost all black with a heavy thick mane and tail. Her name was appropriate because she had a streak of pure white lightning on her forehead.

Cammi sat bareback on the mare first. Lightning took off at a fast pace then stopped short and deliberately dropped her neck. This unexpected move sent Cammi lurching face first onto the ground. But amazingly, the horse had a sense that Jenna was younger and the mare appeared of a gentler nature whenever Jenna was around.

The money Jenna earned from Mrs. Titus bought hay for Lightning. After school each day, Jenna rode Lightning along the roadway and into the forest behind the house. A favorite stopping point was along a stream where Lightning would drink and rest while Jenna relaxed. Lazy autumn afternoons provided ample time for the two of them to explore different trails that wound gradually into mountains where Jenna enjoyed spotting rabbits and deer.

As their first winter in the house approached, Jenna opted not to spend too much time at home when her father was there. He had suddenly become controlling and was oftentimes in a foul and quarrelsome mood. Inside her ten year old mind, Jenna concluded that perhaps she was growing up too quickly to suit her father, because he seemed to direct his bad feelings toward her specifically.

# CATHERINE TREADWELL'S WEDDING

▼

Benny tugged at the stiff starched collar of his shirt. He had never worn formal wear and now he understood why.

Catherine's friend Minnie served as maid of honor. Benny thought she looked cute in her yellow frilly dress. She clung onto his arm, and a couple of times he tried to escape, but she always seemed to find him. Apparently she reckoned if he was her partner for the day, he had damn well better stay within her grasp. The church organist began playing traditional wedding music, and the attendees craned their necks to catch a glimpse of the bride. Feeling awkward, Benny stood motionless at the altar watching Catherine walk slowly down the aisle on her father's arm.

Benjamin had been drinking. The cheeks on his face glowed red, and perspiration dripped around his starched collar. An annoying tic beat continually in his one eye. A hushed whisper among the guests revealed that everyone noticed this embarrassing condition, except for Benny. He stood fixed, entranced with how beautiful and radiantly happy his sister looked. An angel from heaven, he thought, noticing how ravishing she looked in her embroidered lace gown and the Chantilly scarf on her head. All he could think about was how much she deserved this special day, deserved to dream happy dreams for the future. When Benjamin lifted his daughter's veil to kiss her, he fell forward onto her breasts almost causing her to fall backward. Benny quickly came to the rescue and escorted his father to the front pew. Straight away, this caused quiet murmuring to drift into subdued laughter.

After this embarrassment, his mother kept a keen eye on his father. During the reception, she forced him to sit beside her at a table set up on the front lawn of their home. The festivities continued through the rest of the afternoon.

They served madeleine wedding cakes drizzled with chocolate and provided a whiskey punch. Baked ham and yams completed the spread. Aunt Geraldine concocted a lovely pound cake, one large layer adorned with beautiful fall flowers in shades of red, orange, and yellow. An archway decorated with similar fall colors and cornhusks stood near the cake table.

After the last of the guests left, Benny's mother proudly showed off the progress she had made steadying her walk. She entered the house without need of her cane. After his mother's bold performance, Benny happily drove Catherine and William out by Upper Saranac. As a surprise for them, he decorated his car with ribbons and tin cans that he had tied to the rear bumper. The happy couple had reserved a room at the fabulous Wawbeek Inn for three nights. They planned to spend those days relaxing and fishing.

Later that same evening, Benny made his way up to the crew's quarters. He was in desperate need of company and decided it was too early to end the festive atmosphere. Only nine men remained at the quarters including Joe and Lenny. They were the few remaining who had hired on to stay through the winter months.

"Got the happy honeymooners bedded down for the night?" Joe asked.

Benny scratched his head and smiled. "Yeah, they have a few days away, and then it's back to business."

"Got some time for a game of cards?" A couple of men from the back of the room asked in unison.

"Got some of that fine moonshine hidden underneath one of those bunks here?" Benny asked licking his lips.

"More than you can drink in one night for damn sure." Lenny answered.

"Let's go boys, my hands are feeling empty," he said, rubbing his palms together.

Nine months after the couple's wedding, Catherine gave birth to a beautiful baby girl; they named her Minnie after her closest friend. Minnie was a beautiful baby with pink chubby cheeks and Catherine's expressive eyes.

Catherine and William purchased a small home around the bend in the road from the old homestead, but they still spent a lot of time at the Treadwell's place. It was easy for Catherine to leave Minnie in the care of her mother or her aunt Geraldine. They happily volunteered to become babysitters. Seeing her every day, they could not help but fall in love with Minnie, and she grew into a sweet-natured child.

Her most ardent admirer was her grandfather who spent hours doting over and spoiling her. Consequently, when she took her first steps at ten months, she ran those three tiny steps into his waiting arms. During the next few years, Benjamin seemed to have renewed energy and he slowly began to enjoy life again. He started to spend long hours fishing and boating with the child. He made special short treks into the forest with baskets full of goodies in hand. He instructed her on the beauty of the wilderness. When they stopped to picnic, he regaled her with elaborate stories about knights and princesses.

Catherine took control of the mill office and William, who was ensconced in the successful family firm, had precious little time to spend with his daughter. At this time, too, Benny assumed a larger responsibility for running the construction company. He got along well with the subcontractors and crew who admitted that he was easier to deal with than his father was. The crew had become bored with Benjamin's sporadic temper tantrums. Besides, Benny was trusted as being fair and forthright in all of his dealings.

Something in the character of the family changed after Minnie was born. Benny's mother and Aunt Geraldine spent time together behaving more like sisters. Whenever his mother felt up to it, the two women cooked up a large pot of mutton stew. They would bake sumptuous breads and cakes, all the while humming and laughing together. Late summer, the women would spend hours preparing garden vegetables, beans, squash, tomatoes, and peas, for canning. After this chore was completed, they commenced to making jellies and preserving meats. This was such a productive and busy time for everyone that the years flew by quickly.

Grandfather and Minnie sat on the ground under an oak tree in the woods. They had hiked halfway up St. Regis mountain and found a path that led them to a rocky overhang. There they chose to picnic and overlook the lake. Minnie shed her hiking boots, small replicas of her grandfather's boots and massaged her toes. She had walked her limit this morning and could not wait to eat. She was ravenously hungry.

"Tell me the story about Rapunzel again," she said, feeling a bit drowsy.

"You really love that one, don't you? I think it's about ten times now I've told you that story."

"Come on, Grandpop. I really like that story. I like that she grows her hair so long. I wish Mother would allow me to grow mine. She says it's too curly and gets all tangled."

"Let's instead talk about your fifth birthday coming up next month. What do you want your old Grandpop to buy you?"

"Humm, not another doll, that's for sure. Unless you can find for me a Rapunzel doll, which would be nice."

She sat back quietly thinking while her grandfather enjoyed his cigar.

Minnie finally spoke. "You know that old buggy we have behind the barn? Well, I like it and was wondering if you could fix it all up and paint it. Then we can hitch the horses to it and carry all my friends to my birthday party."

"I need to fix the hitch, and it also needs new springs."

"Could you fix it, Grandpop? Then maybe paint it pink and white."

"I could do that. What else would you like, princess?"

"Well, I went to my friend Anne's birthday party, and she had bows tied on all the trees in her yard. I think I would like ribbons hanging from our trees. Then the wind will blow them and they would be so festive. What do you think about that?"

"That sounds like a birthday party fit for Rapunzel herself."

After resting, they hiked back down the mountain. That evening, brimming with excitement, Minnie told her parents about the party she and her grandfather had planned.

"I don't want you to cut my hair until *after* my party," Minnie said. "I want it to grow longer, just like Rapunzel's hair."

"That's just fine, Minnie," Catherine answered.

"And Mama, Grandpop is going to fix up that old buggy we have behind the garage."

"Why, I remember that old buggy from back when I was growing up."

"And he promised to paint it pink and white."

"That should perk up the old buggy," Catherine answered. She knew her daughter could convince Grandpop to do anything she asked.

A month later, the household busily set about preparing for Minnie's birthday party. The event at once became a neighborhood social affair. Every family had received an invitation for the party.

Minnie's grandfather surprised her with the buggy on her birthday morning. He repaired the hitch and springs, painted the wagon box pink and white, and adorned it with pink ribbons and bows. He also presented Minnie with Prince, her very own Shetland pony. Minnie jumped up and down and clapped her hands in glee. The dimples on her cheeks framed her smiling face the rest of the day.

"Uncle Benny," Minnie called. "Come see my new pony that Grandpop gave to me for my birthday."

Benny came out from the barn and inspected the buggy and the pony. He slapped his father on the back.

"That old buggy sure took on another life," he said, laughing at the pink and white colors.

Benjamin set out early to pick up children for the birthday party. Tables were placed in the backyard along the stone wall, and trees were decorated with long pink ribbons that blew in the wind. The women had spent two weeks preparing decorations, food, and candies.

Minnie looked beautiful. Her golden curls were tied back with a pink ribbon that matched her pink long stockings. Her grandmother made her a ruffled white dress. She wore it tied with a pink grosgrain sash at her waist. The birthday girl smiled in pure joy the entire day.

A photographer, commissioned to take photos of the happy event, set up a tripod camera. His photos included a group of girls happily clapping hands around a table piled high with gifts. Then he took a photo of Grandpa leading the pony with Minnie sitting tall in the small leather saddle that her uncle Benny had bought for her. The last photo was beautifully posed. Minnie, surrounded by her family, sat perfectly perched on her grandfather's lap.

The afternoon brought a sudden change in weather. The wind from the north carried along overcast skies and the temperature dropped. Catherine thought it best to return the young guests to their homes before dark.

Benjamin hitched the horses to the buggy and prepared to take the first of the children home.

"Let's see," he asked, "which of you children want to drive home with me and Minnie on our first trip?"

The girls were giggling and playing patty cake when Annie Baker and Mary Rae skipped over and hopped into the cart between Grandpa and Minnie. Benjamin loosened the reins, and as the team started into a full trot, the children's laughter suddenly turned to bloodcurdling screams.

Somehow, the sash on Minnie's dress caught in the back wheel, and she was crushed beneath the moving wagon. The child lay face down on the ground, her blonde curls fanning out around her head. Blood trickled along the dirt in small streams and a thick pool of it, growing larger by the minute, was visible under her small head.

The very first instant Benjamin did not grasp the horror of the situation, and he had a distant detached expression on his face. Finally comprehending, his face contorted into pain and grief. Agonizing sounds emitted from his throat and he fell under the wagon as if in a stupor.

Two hours later, Benjamin lay unconscious in his bed. A physician had administered to him a strong sedative.

Benny sat alone in the night at one of the decorated tables where he remained until past midnight. The pink ribbons blowing wildly in the breeze above his head were now scarcely visible in the darkness. The moon was hidden behind ominous clouds that moved swiftly in the dark sky.

Joe spotted Benny still sitting at the table and came over to join him.

"Take this beer; you look like you need it," Joe offered.

"I'm tired Joe." Benny spoke as if in a trance. "Tired of losing people I love."

Benny held the bottle to his lips and at once downed its contents.

"Do you know where Catherine and William are? I don't hear her screaming anymore," Benny asked of Joe.

"One of the fellas' drove them to the church rectory. I understand they wanted to speak with the minister. They have not come back yet."

"And Father?"

"Dr. Merk came by and administered something to make him sleep. A crazed man, he was."

"My mother, is she still in the house?"

"She and your aunt are together." He studied Benny's face. "I ain't ever seen you looking like this before, Benny."

"I've never felt as helpless as this before."

"Never seen anything quite like it myself," Joe concurred.

"I truly don't know what will become of my father now."

"He sure is in a bad way."

"What the hell do you suppose is going on?" asked Benny. "Everything, including love, dies around here. Both Floyd and Minnie were killed on their birthdays. It ain't right, Joe, it just ain't right."

"I'll stay out here with you tonight. Hopefully the morning sunrise with bring you some peace."

Joe left to fetch two more beers, and they sat together until about five the next morning. Clouds had continued to build. The air rumbled and bolts of lightning streaked the sky as it started to rain hard. The cold weather continued throughout the remainder of the next day.

# BENJAMIN TREADWELL
## DECEMBER 19, 1928

▼

Winter arrived early in December. Four days of blizzard conditions followed by an extreme temperature drop in the early evenings. On the morning of the fifth day, a blinding blaze of sunlight reflected off the white snow. This warmer temperature precipitated a steady drip from icicles that had formed around the roof. Slowly, the trees began to shed the heavy snow.

Benny was relieved to see sunlight when he awoke, so he dressed early. With a full cup of coffee in hand, he anticipated a full day of appointments; appointments he canceled due to inclement weather. He had just sat at the table for some breakfast when his father entered the room.

Benny was surprised to see his father shaved and dressed."What's come over you this morning? Has Mother finally gotten to you, what with her incessant nagging that you bathe and get dressed?"

His father nodded emphatically.

Benjamin had been indisposed since Minnie's death. Most of his meals were brought to his room. His favorite whiskey was ordered, and delivered by the case on a weekly basis from Jeb's store. Many nights Benny could overhear his parents arguing, but he never listened close. Sadly, at this point, he did not much care. But today, unexpectedly his father shows up bathed, shaven, and dressed for the day.

"Do you suppose you and I can get over to see some of the jobs you're presently working on? I would like to spend the day together with you. I have been so damnably depressed lately; I've lost touch with our business."

"Actually I thought you'd never ask," Benny responded. "I'd be happy to. But what do I attribute this change of heart to?"

His father paused, "Tell me first ... have you heard from Catherine or William since they moved back to Malone? I've been wondering how they are getting along since that terrible accident last summer. I've been unable to care about *anything* until now."

"Yes, she has written several times. Last month I telephoned her, and she sounds as though they are doing well ... under the circumstances."

"Do you think she will ever find it in her heart to forgive me?"

"I've told you over and over, Father, she understands it was an accident She feels she and William need more time together, time alone to heal. There are far too many memories here in this house. She told me when I spoke with her last that they are planning to have another child."

"Did they leave to get away from me?"

"Nonsense, what gives you that idea?"

"Just the way she made me feel when she left ... after the ... the horrible accident."

Benny noticed his father's hands shaking uncontrollably. His voice became hoarse and shaky.

"Is this conversation what prompted the changes in your appearance today?" asked Benny. "I mean, I haven't seen you down here in the morning in months."

"Well, frankly, I did need to speak with you, and I want to review and see what the crew is working on. I've cut myself off from any updates, any business news. You've done a fine job of taking over, but frankly I miss working."

He stopped, gathering the courage to continue. "I need to tell you something, Benny. Please don't think I'm crazy. I have never spoken about this to anyone. I was always afraid people would label me a lunatic."

His voice lowered to barely a whisper. "Your grandmother always told me stories, stories about this land, this tract I purchased for a pittance some thirty odd years ago."

Benny listened intently. He watched his father's expressions. His eyes were wild. Benny questioned his father's sanity for the first time.

"When she first moved here, the Indians considered this tract of land evil and malevolent, bathed in blood since the beginning of time. They told your grandmother that the surrounding area was known as The Bloody Hole. They described it as an ancient place where bloodbaths and murder were common-place. A place haunted by the ghosts of murderous spirits that walk the earth hav-ing escaped from the very gates of hell.

"She also heard all kinds of stories from trappers who passed through here. I had always considered it nonsense, until recently. As of late, I have been dwelling on the little time I have left in my life, thinking about the paths I have taken. During the night, I hear voices coming from inside the walls. I feel an icy cold-ness wrap itself around my body and soul, and I fear for the future of everyone who remains in this house."

"Are you sure this has nothing to do with your drinking?"

"Actually, I believe I started drinking because of it. The voices I began hearing started long before the horrible things began to happen. At first, I paid little attention to it. It all began insidiously; I hardly took notice of the changes in myself. But, as I began to realize what was happening, it was too late. Slowly I was engulfed in murderous rages I could not control."

He swallowed hard and continued, "And, sometimes if I am alone in this house, I can feel the enormous power committed to drag me down to their hell-ish beginnings. It is pure, uncontrolled evil, and to me it feels powerfully control-ling and alive. I envision it living and breathing within me and growing stronger by the day."

He stopped to take another deep breath; his eyes were large and bulging reflecting terror. He held his chest with his right hand, gathering the strength to continue. His chest heaved with each labored breath.

"Please forgive me," he said through gasps of air. "I've wanted to leave all of this to you. My legacy, as I envisioned it, was my business and this house for you to enjoy until you die a decrepit old man. I wanted nothing but happiness. I sought it, and craved it for your mother and me. I ask that one day you leave this place, Benny. I couldn't think of you staying here forever. When me and your mother are gone, I plead you move somewhere else so that *it* doesn't drag you down into your own hell."

Benny felt unnerved. "Is it really that bad?" he asked in a lowered tone of voice.

His father could not answer for a few moments. He remained quiet in an attempt to regain control.

"I am tortured by it. Tortured by the voices I constantly hear, by the relentless pursuit of my soul. Lately, I have no release, and a depressing feeling of death and destruction eats away at my gut. It has been constant torture these last years. I never told you, while you were in the army, a partially completed construction building collapsed. It trapped and killed two of our employees."

"It seems there were other things that happened while I was gone."

Benjamin looked at his son as if kicked in the stomach and began to cry. Benny knew his father was thinking of the motorcycle that was discovered in the lake years ago.

"I had to protect you," his father said. "You were very vulnerable during that crisis. I needed to protect you from everything!"

Benny felt a pang of guilt. He had hurt his father with his unkind words.

"Look," Benny said, quickly changing the subject and putting his hand on his father's shoulder. "This is the plan for today. I need to drive over to Gabriel's to pick up some architect plans. Finish having your coffee. I'll be back soon."

Father nodded and forced a weak smile. "Sounds good." He reached over to fill his coffee cup, but his hand shook so visibly it caused the hot liquid to spill onto the table.

"Could you stop at Jeb's store and pick me up some cigars?" his father asked, placing the half-filled cup on the dining room table.

"I sure can. Have to gas up the truck anyway. I'll try to be back in an hour. We can continue our conversation then."

Benny stood. Before he turned to leave, he saw his father reach and pluck a dead leaf from a blooming red geranium plant. The flowering centerpiece seemed out of place against the frosty ice patterns carved into the windowpanes.

Benny pulled into the driveway after running his errands. He stopped the car and paused to stare at the house. He recalled the memory of its frightful appearance on his arrival home from the army seven years before. Aunt Geraldine was upstairs at Mother's bedroom window shaking dust from an old carpet. She pretended not to see him and quickly slammed the window shut and drew the curtains.

Benny found his father still sitting where he had left him at the breakfast room table, hunched over his cup of coffee.

"Thought you'd forgotten about me," his father said.

"Nope, looking forward to spending the rest of the day with you."

Benny placed a new box of cigars on the table.

His father's eyes lit up. "I was hoping you wouldn't forget those."

Benjamin grabbed for the box, opened it, and took out a cigar. He stared at it for a few moments as though it were the most beautiful thing he had ever laid eyes on.

"Well, I'm ready to go if you are, the roads are passable. Has Mother been down for breakfast yet?" Benny asked.

"No, but Geraldine brought breakfast up to her. Your mother is not feeling well this morning."

He rose and put on his coat and gloves "Where do we start?" Benjamin asked.

"These last years have been hard on you. I understand some things have been more painful than any of us thought we could endure," Benny said.

He could hear his father breathing heavily and tears began to well in his eyes.

When father and son arrived home late in the day, the lights were on upstairs. They entered the house and caught a pleasant whiff of beef stew. In the kitchen was a warm loaf of fresh bread under a clean towel on the table. They decided to help themselves.

Halfway through dinner, Benny heard someone walking down the steps. Aunt Geraldine entered the kitchen, her white apron smudged with flour and gravy. She went directly to Father and whispered in his ear.

"Oh, God!" he said. "Does she afford me no peace in this life?"

His shoulders slouched, and he dragged himself up from his chair. Leaving his dinner half-eaten and looking defeated, he scuffled closely behind Aunt Geraldine.

"Your mother needs to see me," he said, turning to look at Benny as he exited the kitchen.

That night the entire household awoke to sounds of men screaming outside. Benny jumped out of bed. An overpowering smell of smoke prompted him to pull on a pair of work pants, and with only his flannel wear and slippers, he raced downstairs and outside into the frigid air.

The crew quarters were ablaze. Black smoke billowed from the roof and windows. Benny quickly ascertained that Lenny and Joe had started a bucket brigade from the water supply in the barn. Men half dressed and barefoot scrambled around in a feeble attempt to save the structure. Suddenly there was a blast. Something had exploded in the downstairs area. Within minutes, the entire building was engulfed in flames. Men with black soot on their faces, many of them bloodied, scrambled to prevent the fire from spreading to the rear of the house.

Benny looked up to see Mother and Aunt Geraldine behind an opened window. They were screaming commands to no one in particular. Father stood behind them, paralyzed by fear. Benny spotted one man, the back of his shirt on fire, running to the front of the house. Benny ran after him, tackled him, and rolled him in the snow. The man screamed in pain, the sickening smell of burned flesh clinging to him. Benny saw another of the workers, his hair singed, and carrying a bucket of water. He was limping due to a misshapen broken leg caused when he jumped from an upstairs window. It took a very short time for the building to be leveled, the fire slowly burning itself out. Townspeople had assembled to pitch in including men from the fire brigade. However, it was too late, the structure was beyond saving.

Joe sat, tears streaming down his face, while a neighbor wrapped his burned arm in gauze. Lenny sat beside his son nursing his boy's severely burned hand. Benny spotted his own father, looking confused, and staring at the trees that bordered the forest. Unbeknownst to Benny, in his father's befuddled mind, he thought he had glimpsed pink ribbons blowing in the breeze.

"What started the blaze?" Benny asked Joe

"We were playing cards one minute, and the next minute we were fighting flames." He gingerly massaged his bandaged arm.

Benny realized he was freezing, and had lost both his slippers, as he slowly limped towards the house. Meanwhile neighbors helped transport the injured to the hospital, while firefighters went around squelching any new fires burning within the perimeter of the structure. They checked the house and noted that the paint had blistered, and in some places, the clapboard siding was burned.

No one slept another wink that night. Benny's feet were numb and he felt grateful for the steaming hot cup of coffee, one of the neighbors placed in his hands. He heard his mother sobbing in the other room, but he thought it best to first thaw his feet in a blanket before going to console her. He cuddled up close to the woodstove where the coals burned a fiery red. Neighbors and fire officials filled the kitchen. Searching the room for his father, and not finding him, Benny went around and thanked everyone. When the kitchen had cleared and everybody had left, Benny saw his father emerge from a dark corner of the pantry, to walk upstairs. He appeared dazed. Benny followed the sound of the floorboards creaking under his father's weight. His father had once again taken refuge in the sanctity of his room.

The following morning, Benny was surprised to see his father dressed, shaved, and apparently ready to face the world.

"Did they discover the origin of the fire?" his father asked.

"We think it was from a kerosene lamp. Joe is being released from the hospital this afternoon. We will find out more from him. The fire department supervisor thinks it may have been electrical, but I have not found any evidence of that yet. Lenny and some of the others were provided lodging at the Mathew's home, but I want Joe to spend some time here with us. He may need some help nursing that injured arm of his."

They heard a train whistle and instinctively knew it was 11:28 in the morning. The train passed through twice a day. They typically set their clocks when the train rolled through town—once in the morning and once at night.

"Do you mind if I drive your old Ford today?" Benjamin asked his son.

"Of course not, where do you plan to go?"

"Maybe go to the hospital to visit some of our friends who were injured in last night's fire."

"Are you sure you'll be okay? It's been awhile since you've been out on your own."

"No, I'm fine, you'll see." He embraced his son with both arms, and then placed a hand on the doorknob. For a moment, he stood silent and stiff, and then turned towards Benny. "Remember the conversation we had a couple of days ago?"

"You mean the one about the demons?"

Father blanched but quickly recovered. "Yes. Don't you ever forget what I've told you," he said in a firm voice as he quickly walked out the door.

A moment later, Benny could hear the sound of his old Ford engine struggling to turn over. He ran outside to tell his father the gas tank was low, but his father had managed to start the car anyway. Benny watched as the old Ford disappeared around the bend.

After visiting friends at the hospital, Benjamin stopped at Ruby's Café and enjoyed a fine dinner of venison stew. Then he headed in the direction of home.

Before he got close to Old Mill Road, Benjamin slowed the car to a stop and engaged the brake. The darkness of the night closed in around him. Patiently, he relaxed back into the car seat and lit a cigar. He relished the first puff, and inhaled it deep into his lungs. The aroma of the cigar filled the car. Circles of smoke floated inside the vehicle like wispy, ghostly figures. He began to feel lightheaded and he smiled, satisfied with the dramatic decision he was finally able to make. He checked the steadiness of his left hand in the moonlight. He was glad he decided to wear his wedding ring tonight. He noticed the tremors had subsided; his hand was recognizably steady now. Playfully he rolled the cigar around in his mouth.

A display of Christmas lights inside Jeb's store caught his attention. The blinking lights and the decorated tree sparkled through the front window. In the background, Benjamin heard the 11:28 train whistle. It was melodic music to his ears. He took another long draw from the cigar and settled more deeply into the worn padded car seat. The train conductor did not see the black car deliberately parked on the tracks, but he thought he saw a tiny red glow from a cigar, as the train obliterated the car.

# BENNY TREADWELL
## GERALDINE

—————————— ▼ ——————————

On Christmas Eve, the town crew deposited the twisted corpse of a vehicle on the far side of the Treadwell's property. It remained there throughout the frozen winter months. After the spring thaw, members from the crew arrived with a backhoe to dig a huge pit at the north end of the property line. Benny watched as they unceremoniously shoved the rusted remains of the vehicle into its final resting place. His father's glasses remained lodged under the front seat and his crushed shoe was wedged inside the mangled front end.

Benny stood as the backhoe pushed and filled the hole with dirt. Inside his mind, he visualized veins of blood dripping down the walls of dirt while the backhoe sealed the pit from the sunlight. He slowly strolled back toward the house and noticed his mother staring down at him from an upstairs window. Her emaciated face appeared sickly and drawn.

He turned to inspect the tree fort that held so many sweet childhood memories. The roof was still intact. Winter storms had taken a toll on the steps and railing that had buckled and broken away, and now lay in a heap on the ground. However, the walls held strong, a monument to Floyd who had spent hours reinforcing them.

He sat under the shadow of the fort in the long grass where wild raspberry lay hidden. He studied the different varieties of weeds that had grown in the crevices of the remaining crew quarters that had burned last year. He allowed his mind to span the years he had spent in this house, and before long, he dropped his head to his knees and sobbed.

That evening at dinner, he sat across from Aunt Geraldine and Catherine. His sister's body was beginning to bulge under the weight of her pregnancy. They enjoyed a fine dinner of veal stew with shallots and wine sauce and attempted to make small talk. Unfortunately, the horrors of the last few months created uncomfortable, stilted conversation.

"This is great Geraldine; my father always enjoyed it when you served this meal," Benny said casually.

Aunt Geraldine scrunched her lips and obviously forced an answer. "Glad you like it. Suppose we could get some venison next fall?"

"Suppose that's a possibility."

Benny smiled, recalling all the years of exciting hunting expeditions.

"What time are you leaving in the morning, Catherine?" Benny asked.

"The minute William arrives to pick me up." Benny pretended not to hear the indifference in her voice.

"It's been good for Mother to see you again, now especially that you're pregnant."

She smiled. It was still her smile, but stiff and no longer mirrored joy.

"William has become so busy. I hope one day that he can take some time off to visit with you. When he comes to pick me up tomorrow, he only has an hour to spare before we have to head back again." She paused and turned to Benny. "I've been thinking that you're going to have to get someone qualified to care for mother."

Aunt Geraldine heard this remark and became belligerent. "Haven't I been a fair to middling nurse for your mother?"

"Yes, but with her condition worsening by the day, I believe she needs full time assistance," Catherine said firmly.

"I've been thinking along those lines too," Benny interjected, ignoring his aunt's retort.

"We can write up an advertisement in the morning and publish it here in the *Enterprise* and also in the Malone newspaper," Catherine suggested.

Benny nodded agreement. Aunt Geraldine abruptly rose from her chair and began to remove the dishes from the table. She had grown much heavier, and her cumbersome body moved slowly. It appeared her arthritic knee was bothering her, because she limped out of the dining area.

When Aunt Geraldine was out of earshot, Catherine asked in a whisper, "How on earth do you stand it here?"

"What? Geraldine? I pay her no attention."

"No, I don't mean her. I mean this house! It gives me the willies. I need to get away from here, it's stifling. Every now and again I hear strange noises."

"What! Are you complaining about the proverbial haunted mansion?" He laughed.

"It's not funny, Benny, are you immune? Don't you feel it too?" She was obviously agitated.

"I suppose sometimes." He shrugged. "Two days before Father died, he told me that he believed this house tormented and drove him to the brink of madness. Frankly, I don't know what to believe anymore. What I do know is that I am so busy right now I can't see straight."

The tone of his voice began rising uncontrollably. "I have no place to house the crew. I've had to rent whatever is available until we can rebuild new quarters. Besides all of that, my convalescent mother requires constant care. That doesn't sound to me like I have time to think about whatever unholy ghosts pace the floors around here!"

"You're getting as crazy as Father was," she said, and stood to leave the table. But feeling faint, she immediately sat herself back down in the chair. Benny watched his sister, his demeanor expressing impatience.

"You know, Catherine, you can say what you want, but don't accuse me of *that*."

"That! Do mean accuse you of getting as crazy as Father?"

The conversation was interrupted by a constant loud banging on the ceiling. The noise came from a cane striking the floor in their mother's room upstairs. Mother had obviously overheard the argument and it was her way of intervening. Catherine regained her composure and softly rubbed her belly after she felt a sharp kick from her unborn child.

"Benny, let's not allow this to get out of hand. All I wanted to convey to you is that when I come here I get the feeling this place reeks of death. It's as though there is a lingering sadness—a memory stored in every room of somebody who died. Every wall has witnessed cries of grief and horror and held the dead within its perimeter. I cannot stand it any longer. I can promise you that after tonight, only William will return here. If you ever decide you want to see me again, come to my home. It is a much happier place than this dreary, drafty old house."

Early the next morning, William arrived. Catherine was unable to enjoy breakfast because she was feeling somewhat nauseated. William and Benny stole a few moments alone while packing the car.

"This fall I expect some company from the south of the state to visit me for a hunting party," Benny began. "Every other time we've planned a hunting trip something comes up and we've had to cancel. I will let you know our plans, and I hope you can join us. By that time your child will be born, and I am sure Catherine can spare you for a long weekend."

"Count me in brother-in-law. Surely by that time I will be in desperate need of some time away from home." They both laughed.

Benny remained outside to see them off. William promised to visit again after the baby was born, and Benny gave his sister a big hug and wished her a speedy birth.

"Please telephone me as soon as he or she is born." He waved good-bye.

Benny paused a moment to inspect the business sign, which stood at the end of the driveway. It read *Benjamin Treadwell & Son, Contractor*. He made a mental note to have it repainted with his name only. It was time to move forward.

Reentering the silent house, he felt a cold damp draft and an eerie foreboding of danger, so he built a roaring fire in the fireplace. He remained sitting in his favorite chair, in front of the fireplace until the temperature in the room rose to a feverish pitch. He needed to decide how to facilitate a way to move away from the house with his mother in such a needy condition.

However, the next morning brought another catastrophe.

"Mother, you're being obstinate!" Benny did not often raise his voice, especially to his mother, but his frustrations were wearing on his nerves. His mother lay in bed clutching the Bible to her chest. Her upper lip was set defiantly in a paper-thin line across her face. Her jaws clamped tight and her eyes blazed fire, tenaciously unwilling to yield to her son's ridiculous demand.

"You must accept a twenty-four hour nurse. The ad is in the newspaper, and I have interviewed several applicants. I will do my best to find someone you won't be able to chase away in one short month."

Sometimes she is so damned frustrating.

On his way out of her bedroom door, he heard her hoarse whispered rebuttal. "I do not know what's so wrong with the care I get from Geraldine."

He stopped and turned to her, his face flushed. "Dammit, Geraldine can barely get around anymore, no less pick you up out of your bed." He reached for the doorknob and slammed the door behind him. He knew he would acquiesce to her demand simply because it was easier, so the existing arrangement stayed in place one more month.

A week later, Benny arrived home to a dark and silent house. From the driveway, he caught a whiff of burned cookies. He ran into the dark kitchen stumbling over something lying on the floor. Aunt Geraldine lay dead.

After the doctor arrived, and the body was turned over to be removed, Benny smiled. His aunt still had traces of flour clinging to her face when she died. The ever present pot holder remained as if frozen in her hand—a death grip. Suddenly, from the ceiling, he heard his mother banging her cane on the floor. She had awakened from her afternoon nap and was stunned to hear from Benny the news of Geraldine's sudden demise.

The family buried Aunt Geraldine in the graveyard beside her son, Floyd. It had been years since Benny had visited the gravesite. Wilted flowers remained in mute testimony of Geraldine's last visit to her son's grave.

Benny drove home in silence and walked immediately into his aunt's private living quarters. It was akin to entering a tomb; she had sealed herself off from the outside world for years. Inside, Benny saw numerous photographs of Floyd, black and white reminders of the happy child. In one photograph, Floyd was smiling, a cute mischievous twinkle in his eyes. Another showed him to be about two years old and sitting on his mother's lap. A strange man, most likely Floyd's father, stood stiffly proper beside her, his hand resting on Geraldine's left shoulder.

The room reeked of candle wax, and Benny noticed that in every available space remained a mound of melted wax. He carefully studied the room. To his amazement, he saw the curtains, yellowed and rotten, hanging in shreds. The windows were double shaded to keep light from filtering in. He dropped down heavily on the bed. His eyes were drawn to a pine chest near the bed. He opened the lid. It was filled to the top with yearly journals dating back to 1900. Benny lit a kerosene lamp and lay back upon his aunt's lumpy pillow, his knees drawn up.

The writings from 1914, the year Floyd died, were filled with illegible scribbles and pages were ripped from the binding.

*November 1914*

*I walked into the forest, the air was frigid, and I wore only my nightshirt. The sound of the stream running softly through the woods caught my attention, and I went to it hoping to see you sitting there again. Why don't you show yourself to me like you did last month? It was a magical vision; the bright moonlight focused on you with sparkles of color. Seemingly as though viewing you in another dimension and peering through melted icicles. You know how much your beloved mother misses you.*

*April 1915*

*I submerged myself in the icy cold water of the stream, feeling relief and deliverance from my insane thoughts, now I am thinking clearer. I am always wondering why you were snatched from me, snatched from my arms. Were you taken away to punish me for something? I don't know what I did to deserve such pain and anguish.*

*June 1915*

*I was astonished to see your spirit rising from the muddy creek. You almost resembled Father Neptune as your body slowly rose, dripping wet with muddy slime clinging to you. I screamed, but knew you would not harm me, your beloved mother. I wanted to tell you that I suspect it was not Benny who is guilty of killing you. I have many dark suspicions. You came to me because you somehow must know the truth in my suspicions. Forces point me in all diverse directions. I cannot allow anyone in this house to suspect my energies are focused in my pursuit to discover whoever is truly responsible for your death.*

Benny continued reading. Horror filled the passages.

*October 31, 1915*

*I have been reading many books that lie hidden away in my room. I consulted with one popular piece devoted to witchcraft. It prompted me to shed my nightshirt in the blackness of the forest, calling together the dark Spirits of the Long Dead to come to me. They promise me solace and comfort. They offer to take me to the Gates of Hell and view the heinous creatures that reside in the place that we all refer to as hell. Inside myself, I am already there. I beg to see your last moments on this earth. I feel so helpless in the darkness of the night. The darkness accentuates my fears and suspicions. It causes me to feel a hallow emptiness, and I cannot fill the void in any manner.*

*January 10, 1916*

*I went to the stream, but it had changed into a small brook bubbling through the new snowfall. It meandered slowly down from the mountain peaks. Pretty soon, I will be unable to view it because of the amount of snow storms we have, and then it will bubble away unseen, hidden underneath its white blanket. That's the way I see you. You are still here, but unseen, hidden behind the dark screen of the world of the dead.*

*I often can feel your presence while I am in your room. Are you looking for something special here? Something you hid away a long time ago? I want to see your sweet face again. Show yourself to me. I wait for that vision every waking moment.*

*I cannot allow anyone else in this house to obtain any knowledge about the dark creatures that inhabit this house! It is my secret! The creatures I see are alive, and squirming in a chasm. They live in a huge yawning hole that swirls down into the fiery core of the earth. Elizabeth and Benjamin would be too frightened, so I keep the creatures only for me to know about and understand.*

*A little mouse ran past me to hide under your bed. Remember how you used to giggle while playing with them in the barn. Sometimes, when I am alone in this house, I can hear your giggle; the sound of it overwhelms me with happiness and joy.*

*March 10, 1917*

*Benny left to visit New York City or somewhere. I am glad he is out of the house. Now I can turn my attentions to my sister and her husband. I have overheard something that leads me to believe they are hiding the truth behind their stupid expressions of hatred for one another.*

*I plan to work very hard on my new teachings of the occult. During my séances I try hard to bring you back from the grave, but I don't know why I have only seen you by the creek. Please show yourself to me so I can see your sweet face again. I miss you so very much. I cry myself into exhaustion every night.*

*June 19, 1918*

*They found the damnable thing the boat struck! It gives me a lot to ponder. I have a good idea how it got in the water. Damn the thing! And damn the person who put it there! They will have hell to pay!*

*July 25, 1918*

*Last night, the spirits were able to lead me into the darkest depths of hell. I witnessed acts so heinous and frightening that I cannot describe and cannot write down the vile acts. Horrible things, deaths by beheading and red men slicing off scalps with hatchets, murder in cold blood and cannibal rituals, slaughter of innocent souls. There were other things so vile I cannot write them onto this page. They promised me if I stood witness to this, I would one day be granted my wish to witness your last moments on this earth, moments where I could have saved you. Moments I could not have witnessed before my transformation into their servant.*

*October 15, 1918*

*I know now who really murdered you. Murdered you in cold blood! I will be sure they never suspect I know what happened. I will continue to pursue their souls with every breath I breathe. I will be sure they pay for their evil deeds. I screamed for retribution, and it will be sweet when it comes. They all see me as their innocent servant, forever happily cooking and cleaning house for them. It is a wonderful illusion, because it grants me access to all conversations and events that stir their own happiness. This enables me to target their weaknesses, overwhelm their spirit, and in the end, control their souls.*

*February 13, 1919*

*It was my long awaited night of enlightenment. I was finally allowed to stand witness to those last moments you spent on earth. I saw your head bloodied with the open gash still bleeding in the murky dark water. But, you were still alive, screaming, though I could not hear the words. Were you calling out to me to save you? I could swear it seemed like you were calling for your dear mother. Now I know, as I had believed all this time, that in your last struggling moments on this earth, you screamed out for me alone, and no one else.*

*April 1, 1921*

*I thought it an April fool story that Benny is coming home again, but I have been reassured that it is true. I'm glad you are happy to have him back here with you so close by. They all happily plan for a future wedding, never giving an inkling of a thought that you have suffered so intensely. How can they experience happiness when my soul is lost and still so miserable? For this and this alone I wish them all damnation. May they continue to rot in the hell that is this house!*

*November 15, 1921*

*I am glad the wedding festivities are past. There was so much hustle and bustle about, and they kept me so busy, treating me like a servant again, baking and doing all the work that requires full concentration, persnickety details. I pretend that I am enjoying it all because it allows me access to their dreams, so I can destroy them in the end.*

*June 14, 1922*

*Catherine gave birth to a baby girl today. The baby arrived slightly early, they say, but I think they fornicated and conceived the child before the wedding. The baby is a wormy little thing who resembles her father. Benjamin gazes at her asleep in her cradle; his eyes aglow, as if in lust for this granddaughter of his. It disgusts me completely that he should shower so much attention on this screaming infant. It disgusts me that he be allowed access to any happiness. Just when I thought he was a broken man.*

Benny dozed off for a short time. But when a journal slid from his grasp and fell to the oak floor, he awoke with a fright. He surmised it was dawn, and he felt an urgent need for a cup of coffee to clear the cobwebs from his seemingly drugged mind. He knew his mother would soon be stirring and banging on the floor wanting her morning rituals. He postponed reading the remaining journals for another night. He felt he needed to assimilate the information he had already read.

Two days later, Benny purposefully came home early so he could read the remaining journal he found so disturbing. He now was convinced that his aunt Geraldine had been stark raving mad.

He entered her musty smelling quarters and ripped the shoddy coverings from the windows. Only the smallest particles of sunlight had entered the room in years. The bright sunlight now filtered in the room and revealed dirty walls and old and decrepit furniture.

Benny carried with him a small wooden box where he carefully packed the journals he had read. The unread journals he piled beside him and skimmed through them noticing the same insane ranting that filled each of the others. As he skimmed through the most recent years, her writings became more disturbing so he targeted several passages to study.

*May 18, 1923*

*The child they call Minnie is doted upon unmercifully. I think she would rather be left alone sometimes. Her mother fixes her hair as best she can, because it is thin, wispy hair that hangs in tangled curls. Sometimes I pinch her to cause her some pain. As always, they comfort and snuggle her to make the tears go away, without knowing the origin of her pain.*

*Christmas Day, 1923*

*They give her so many toys and luxuries; treat her like royalty. Whenever you and I made Christmas together, there were never so many gifts under the tree. I am thinking that you need a playmate, and how much better it would be for you to have someone in the family be there with you. Catherine can always have another baby. I think about this every night, and hope to hear you giggle again. It seems to have faded. I rarely hear you anymore playing upstairs or by the creek.*

*June 30, 1926*

*I have cast a spell, and I think it is working. I followed the directions passed to me from a secret source, a practicing witch who lives nearby. I want to be sure that when I die, my soul will remain trapped here with yours—all souls living in this house forever, walking the floors for eternity. Our rotting, stinking bodies will remain underground in the cemetery, but I plead for my soul to remain here with you.*

*You gave me a sign that you think it would be a fine idea if Minnie came to you. I had a dream where you cradled a baby in your arms, and when you smiled at me, the baby suddenly became a dark growling wolf with long fangs dripping blood. The wolf threatened to destroy you, but you killed it with one swipe of your hand. The wolf's head split open and brains spilled from the opening. The wolf corpse fell to the ground and transformed itself into Minnie. She lay dead, but you lifted her withered body to me and smiled as if to accept the approval of her death. You have given me approval from the grave, and I promise to carry out your directive.*

*June 12, 1927*

*Her birthday is Monday, but they made a party for her today so that the children from the whole neighborhood could come. What ostentatious trappings for one spoiled child. Her grandfather presented her with a Shetland pony, brown with a blond mane and tail. When my chance finally arrived, it was so easy and worked so well even I was surprised. I only had to tie her dress ribbons to the wheel of the buggy. I tied them so tight that there was no chance of saving the little wench. When Benjamin drove the buggy away, she was dashed to the ground and was dead!*

*Just like the wolf, whose brains you spilled in my dream. It was the same. And it was instantaneous death with no cuddling and coddling. They were helpless to save her life! In my mind, I saw you hold out her body and present it to me. You then smiled, just like in my dream. It was retribution to perfection, and it was so easy. I am sure that the next time I hear you giggling Minnie will be with you. Right now, in my imagination, I can see both of you playing together by the creek. Today, the Spirit of Satan blesses me!*

Benny retched and then vomited all over the bed. Recovering, he immediately ran to the barn, grabbed an ax, and destroyed all the furniture in Aunt Geraldine's room. Building a fire in the fireplace, he slashed all of his aunt's clothes and tossed them into the roaring fire. Crazed, he continued to search for anything he could remember her ever having touched when she was alive.

His mother began banging the floor with her cane. Benny also damned her in his fit of insanity. Screaming in agonizing horror, he threw some of the unread journals in the fire. He only preserved some small trinkets that had belonged to Floyd, including the photograph of him standing alone.

Benny made a promise to himself never to reveal the contents of the journals to Catherine. The deed was done. It would cause her too much pain to know that Minnie was murdered. He carefully laid the box containing some of the journals he had read in a closet in his bedroom.

The next morning he arranged for his workers to strip and paint Aunt Geraldine's quarters as an effort to erase any memory of her from the house. Anything that she had used in the kitchen Benny smashed or buried. All of her favorite pots and pans were thrown into a pit and covered with a backhoe. He felt it was akin to an exorcism; as he cleansed from the house any trace from this insane murderer.

The following week he surveyed the spanking clean, newly painted rooms. He felt positive he had accomplished what he set out to achieve, that is until he went to bed and closed his eyes. As he tossed, turned, and tried to sleep, he distinctly heard the rattling of heavy pots and pans moving downstairs in the kitchen. Horrified he once again smelled the distinctive odor of burned cookies.

# THE CHANGES

▼

"Keep shoveling, dammit!" Michael screamed, his face flushed and contorted in anger.

"Calm down, Michael. It's only figgin' coal we're unloading."

Renee started to whimper, her lip quivered attempting to squelch her tears.

"I've got to go to the bathroom," Cammi said, and she leaped off the edge of the pickup.

"Hurry up! I want to be done with this job," Michael hollered.

"Well, you didn't have to go get a full ton of coal and expect the four of us to unload it like some dime laborers."

"It was free, and it will help to keep all of us warmer this winter."

She marched to the house and was astonished to see her reflection in the window. She resembled a coal miner. Her hair was unwashed and disheveled; coal dust clung to her face and clothes.

He reminds me of a damn drill sergeant!

Suddenly Renee started to howl. Cammi rushed back outside to see blood pouring from her ankle.

"Daddy hurt me," she yelled at the top of her lungs, as she jumped into Cammi's open arms.

Michael kept his head down to avoid Cammi's cold stare, and continued to shovel, as she quickly rushed Renee into the house.

"What happened?" she asked her daughter when they were alone.

"Daddy hit me with the shovel because I was tired and sat down to rest."

The wound was jagged and ugly, but nothing that needed stitches. Cammi held ice compresses to stop the bleeding. Renee had her ankle raised on the sofa arm when Jenna stormed into the house.

"Sometimes I hate him!" Jenna said between clenched teeth.

"Now what's up with you?"

Jenna started to cry. Cammi noticed how sensitive she had become around her father lately, but she had dismissed it as the beginning of puberty.

"He's mean! He was never mean before. He started yelling at me, so I came inside. Let him do the shoveling himself. He's stronger than all of us!"

Jenna headed toward the bathroom to shower. "You know, Mom, I think Dad is going crazy," she said before slamming the bathroom door. Cammi could distinguish mournful sobbing above the sound of the running shower.

"Why did Daddy hurt me?" Renee innocently asked.

"I'm sure he didn't really mean to, honey," Cammi answered back, not believing her own words.

The phone rang.

"Will you be all right alone on the couch?"

With a pitiful expression, Renee assured her mother she would be okay. She held onto her now bandaged leg.

"Oh Lou, I'm so glad you called now, I so needed to talk to someone."

Unexpectedly, Cammi began to sob.

"Cammi, what's going on there?" said Lou.

"Renee hurt her leg."

After Cammi explained what had happened, Lucille became incensed. "That ignorant brother of mine may be lacking finesse in some ways, but I have never seen him behave mean or vicious toward anyone, least of all to you and the girls."

"Lucille, this past winter he's become depressed and sullen, and he always appears angry. I mean, all these years married to him, he's *never* acted like this. I have to believe the hard winter had something to do with it."

Relieved to be able to unburden herself, Cammi proceeded. "I mean, sometimes the temperature dropped to horrendous levels below zero. We had to have a heater installed in our car just so it would start in the morning."

"And … what else?"

"We've all had to move downstairs to sleep, because we couldn't afford to heat the upstairs bedrooms any longer. What with the cold, Michael could only work indoors. He has some major construction jobs under contract, but he can't begin any of them until spring breaks and the lakes thaw."

"I had no idea, Cammi. I was wondering why I hadn't heard from either of you in such a long time."

"That's only the tip of the iceberg," Cammi began. "We had a bad storm and our electric was out for so many hours that the pipes in the kitchen sink burst. Believe it or not, a kitchen towel was frozen to the floor! For three nights, we all slept on the floor in front of the fireplace because it was the only heat we had. Of course, having to make all of the repairs here, Michael lost quite a few days at work. That made us go from bad to worse and from poor to poorer."

"What can I do to help?"

"I don't know at this point. If I had some money, I'd drive down to Long Island with the children and visit with my family. But I can't even afford to do that right now."

Cammi noticed Renee had dozed off on the couch.

"I have an idea," Lucille said. "Let me see if there is some work available around here. Maybe a change of scenery would be good for Michael. I mean, he can stay with us and work. At least make some money to send home to you."

"I don't know how we can actually exist with him being gone. I mean, I cannot manage to maneuver the snow blower in the event we get a spring storm. We would be trapped in the house until it melts. Besides, there is no talking to him now with the moods he's in."

"Wait just one minute, Cammi. You're sounding tremendously overwhelmed."

"I *am* overwhelmed! The latest thing around here is, when the girls and I leave to run an errand, we get home and Michael is outside in the snow sitting on the steps. It doesn't matter how cold it is, there he sits waiting for us to come home. He says he hears voices in the house whenever he is alone. Claims to hear scratching noises coming from inside the walls. I thought maybe it was mice or rats, because frankly I don't hear anything myself. Then of course, there is a lady in the kitchen that I sense. But, she appears harmless to me."

"Wait a minute. What lady in the kitchen? Are you all going batty?"

"No, really, we're all okay," Cammi reassured her sister-in-law. "It started soon after we moved in. I only sense her in the pantry and kitchen area. Sometimes I see someone from my peripheral vision, but when I turn in her direction, no one is there. I envision her wearing a black dress, and she has her hair pulled away from her face. I can sense her working alongside me as I cook and clean."

Cammi paused to question her own sanity. "Do I sound batty, too?"

Lucille sighed long and hard without a reply.

"Something else started about a week ago," Cammi continued. "I woke up with someone staring at me while I was asleep. It was Renee. She told me there was a *lady* sitting on her bed. Then I went with her to her room, but of course, no one was there. Each night since, Renee has come into our bedroom and dragged me back into her room to meet the *lady*. I don't know what to think about this newest phenomenon."

"Are you all back sleeping in your own bedrooms now?" Lucille sounded disturbed by the unusual conversation and revelations.

"Yes, now that spring is thankfully around the corner. We are already preparing for our survival next winter. That's exactly why Michael went out and loaded up a ton of coal. He says we have to be more prepared this year, now that we've experienced how really severe the winters can be."

"Does it look like there might be some relief for you in sight?" Lucille asked.

"There is one thing that might perk Michael up. Next month, our friends Ron, Marie, and their sons are planning to visit us. You remember Ron? He helped us move up here."

Cammi heard the outside door open and presumed it was Michael. She covered her mouth over the receiver and whispered into the phone. "Got to go, I'll call you as soon as possible."

She hung up quickly, hoping she did not leave Lucille worrying too much about the sanity and well-being of her family.

# THE VISIT

▼

"I'm so glad the weather broke for your visit. Winter seemed like it would go on forever up here. At least you brought springtime temperatures from Long Island with you." Cammi covered the peeled potatoes with warm water and placed the pot on the stove to cook. "Everyone loves mashed potatoes with meat loaf."

"Your meatloaf smells so great, it's making me hungry! How long do you think it will take the kids to feed Lightning?" Marie asked.

"Oh, not too long, Jenna has that chore down pat. But, I think they might go on an adventure together up to the old clubhouse behind the old Huczek house when they're done. Jenna and Renee like to play there. It's an abandoned building that's falling apart, but I know my girls would love to take your boys up there and show them around."

Marie sat in an old rocker in the kitchen. "Gosh, honey, we've all missed you in the neighborhood. Ron swears that when he retires from the department, he wants to move up here. He has been bragging about the lush forests, the mountains, and the scenery. Now I can see he was right on, it's gorgeous, and you're lucky to be living here."

Cammi smiled, not willing to divulge the sordid details of the changes that had taken place in her life since they had moved upstate.

"I miss living on Long Island also. Life is a bit harder here because the winter's are so long and the cold, well that's another story."

"What's wrong with Michael?" Marie asked. "I mean I never remember him so distracted and miserable. He just isn't himself. I had always envied the relationship you both had together, but, it's obvious something is bothering him."

"Is it really so obvious?"

"With us it is, remember we knew him before you two moved up here. He was always so fun loving. That's why Ron suggested they go out fishing today. He thought it would be good for just the guys to spend some time together. Ron's worried about him. We sat up late last night and talked about it."

"Michael has been behaving like this all winter," Cammi began. "It started soon after we moved in. Do you remember how fastidious and primping Michael always was? I mean I had to actually fight for a tiny view in the bathroom mirror every morning. Then suddenly he just lies around and doesn't shave or wash up. One time, he fell asleep on the couch fully dressed. After he woke up, he left for work wearing the same wrinkled smelly clothes. It's just not like him to do that."

She sat down in a chair and continued."But, it's more than that, Marie. It's the way he behaves toward us. I can see it has affected Jenna a lot. You remember how she was always hanging on her Dad? Well, that's changed now. Sometimes when he's home, she goes to the barn and doesn't come home until bedtime. Renee acts as though she's afraid of him too, so she avoids him."

"To what do you attribute these changes?"

"Personally, I'm stumped. He absolutely refuses to discuss it, just flat out rants, and raves if I broach the subject. Lately, he frightens me too. I was comfortable with the man I married. Right now, he behaves like somebody else. He has hurt the kids a few times. One time he almost hit me too, but he caught himself in time, and stormed out of the room."

"Jeez, now you're really scaring me, Cammi. It's actually worse than I thought."

"And believe me; it's getting worse by the day."

The next day, Ron and Marie took a short sightseeing tour to Whiteface Mountain.

"We love this part of the world!" Marie exclaimed to her friends when they returned.

"Now you understand why we couldn't wait to move here," Cammi said. "Except for the cold and the fifty feet of snow it would be perfect."

"And a lack of insulation in the attic and walls does nothing to keep out Jack Frost," Michael chimed in from the other room. "I plan to insulate the attic this summer, that's the next chore on my long list of things to do. And that should help keep you warm," he said, turning to Cammi.

"By the way," Marie interrupted, "we stopped at the beautiful stone church that's located on the road to your house, and we noticed a large monument in the cemetery. It was marked the Treadwell gravesite. You mentioned that's the family who originally built this place."

"Calvin, the creep who sold us this place, said that Benjamin Treadwell built the house for his family around the turn of the century," Cammi said. "Some years later, Calvin was hired to take care of this house for Benny Treadwell. Then, I guess Calvin went and purchased it from him. Though I don't know how he could afford it, Calvin seems so poor and illiterate."

Cammi continued. "One of my neighbors told me that Benny is still alive and living somewhere in the Lake Placid area with his wife, Clara."

"Interesting, and you've never met them?" Marie asked.

"No, but an old man stopped by here on his motorcycle one day, a beautiful Harley at that." Cammi paused and grabbed some plates to set the table.

"He told us he used to care for the team of logging horses. His name was Joe, and he said he still keeps a close friendship with Benny Treadwell and his wife."

Together Cammi and Marie began to position the silverware beside each plate.

"Joe did say something I thought was really strange. He admitted that the house still spooks him as it did when he was young. He refused to come in to sit down and talk, because he always felt uncomfortable whenever he was inside."

"What else?" asked Marie, mesmerized by the implications that the house was haunted.

"He told us about the night of the fire when the crew quarters burned to the ground. You know the old crumbling foundation out back? Anyway, he rolled up his sleeves and showed us the scars on his arms from that blaze."

"Well, that's interesting," said Marie. "We walked into the cemetery today just to kind of poke around, because I remembered last night you gave me a little information about the Treadwell family."

Cammi nodded as she placed glasses next to each plate.

"I guess this guy Benjamin Treadwell had a father who was killed in the American Civil War," Marie continued.

Cammi expressed surprise."Really, is he buried there? The guy from the civil war, I mean."

"No, but there is something written about him on the tombstone." Marie removed a tattered piece of paper from her pocket where she had scribbled down the inscription from the tombstone.

"It reads *Benjamin Treadwell son of Malcolm and Mildred Treadwell*. Then there is an inscription that reads *Malcolm Treadwell died April 18, 1863, buried in Washington, DC.*"

"What's his name again?" Cammi asked incredulously.

"Malcolm Treadwell is the father of Benjamin, the man who built the house."

"I shiver every time I hear the name Malcolm."

"Why?"

"A hangover from a long-ago dream I had, and a very scary psychic experience with an old Ouija board."

Overhearing this remark by his wife, Michael's face contorted. "What Ouija board experience did you have?" he demanded. "I don't know anything about that! How come you never told me?"

"I never told you about it, Michael, because it happened a long time ago, and at the time it was insignificant."

"Secrets, I hate secrets," he said, losing his temper. He got up from the next room and stomped toward her. He put his face inches from hers.

"Secrets, how many more secrets do you have? I'm your husband; I am supposed to know everything!"

Embarrassed and unnerved, Cammi began to cry. Michael stormed out of the house. He got into his car, started the engine, and squealed out of the driveway.

"Whew! What was that about?" Ron asked.

"He's like this all the time. Wound up like a rubber band so tight he's ready to snap," cried Cammi. "Honestly, I don't know how long we can put up with his ranting and raving. It's affecting all of us."

"You think it might have started when you moved into this house?" Ron asked.

"Maybe. I never saw any changes in him prior to our move."

"Is he overburdened on the job?"

"He hardly had any work this winter."

"Well, that in itself might do it. Maybe he's worried about the finances."

The three adults sat up late into the night and talked. Finally, shortly after midnight, Michael arrived home. He apologized to Cammi. It was extremely obvious to her and the others that he had spent the last hours sitting in a bar drinking. Ron and Marie exchanged quizzical glances with one another, seemingly concerned about Michael and Cammi's relationship.

They soon all retired to bed, but Cammi could not sleep. Restless, she lay under the covers staring at the ceiling. Michael had passed out and was snoring loudly.

She needed some time to think, but intuition told her the answers were within her grasp. She could not put her finger on it, but something she heard tonight led her to think in a new direction. The answer to all her problems lay hidden inside this house.

Suddenly, she became frightened. No, not just frightened, she became terrified. She sensed a remote possibility that in all these years her life was more than just a series of coincidences. Michael was the one who made the decision to move upstate and into this house. He was the one who was so gung ho about the place early on, finding it first and then buying it impulsively.

Maybe the Fanelli family was fulfilling an obligation to destiny. Whose destiny? She was not sure. What she now slowly realized was that when the Ouija board called out to her she became a part of a puzzle. But, now she believed the piece of the puzzle wasn't her specifically.

She concluded that it was most likely Michael who was destined to live in this house. A coincidence perhaps that the name Malcolm would pop up, the soldier in her dream who said *they want you back!* Maybe Michael *belonged* here. She wondered what truths would eventually be revealed. How could she conceivably understand such outlandish supernatural happenings?

# JENNA AND MICHAEL

▼

The next month, Cammi was forced to make a dramatic decision. It was not one she had chosen lightly, but she could not continue to live in the house. The seemingly mild paranormal occurrences were getting on her family's nerves, and she felt positive it was unsafe and unhealthy for the children. The time was right to break the news to Michael of her leaving, and she hoped for a mutual agreement.

She was positive Michael would throw a fit, so she decided to discuss her determined resolution with him on a weekend when both girls were invited to a sleepover birthday party. It would make things easier if the girls were not around to witness the inevitable argument that was sure to ensue.

The contracted construction work at Santa's Workshop was completed within the allotted timeframe. Then within the course of a few months, all of Michael's prospective contracts were cancelled. Cammi was aware that times were going to get even tougher financially. It was during this bleak period filled with angst that Cammi sought to pursue some positive changes.

She arranged with her parents to loan her a bit of money to enable a move back to Long Island with or without Michael. She knew an ultimatum would be difficult for Michael to accept, but she hoped he would recognize the rationale for her decision and follow her and the children.

Even though living in the house terrified him, something unreasonable within him clung to the idea of ownership of the property. She firmly believed that he would eventually concede to her wishes. It was during this volatile period, that one weekday morning Cammi awoke to her daughter's screams.

"Mom! I need you down at the barn!" Jenna hollered and rushed into Cammi's room.

Cammi jumped from the bed and slid into her slippers.

"Lightning's sick. She's rolling around in her stall. I went to the barn to feed and water her this morning and she's making funny grunting noises. Her belly is swollen really big and she keeps kicking at it."

Cammi gave her daughter a comforting hug and searched for the jeans she had casually tossed over a bedroom chair the night before.

"Sounds to me like she has a bellyache, honey. I'll call Mrs. Titus and see what she suggests we do to help Lightning feel better."

Cammi rushed to pull up and zipper her jeans, and grabbed a flannel shirt from the closet.

A moment after her phone conversation with Mrs. Titus, Cammi sat down beside Jenna in the living room.

"We need to try to walk Lightning to prevent her from thrashing," Cammi said calmly.

A loud crash of thunder caused them both a fright. Bright light flashed in the windows.

"The storm's overhead, so we'll wait a couple of minutes, honey. I'll make you some oatmeal the way you like it best with cinnamon and sugar."

"I wish it weren't raining so hard outside, Mom. The longer I stay away from her, the bigger the chance she might hurt herself."

Cammi listened to the heavy rain pelt the tin roof of the overhang.

"Try to eat something, please." Cammi gingerly placed a bowl of oatmeal in Jenna's lap.

"I'll wake your father up and have him call the school to excuse you for today."

Jenna put a large spoonful of oatmeal in her mouth, but spit it out into a napkin and put the bowl into the sink to wash. Cammi realized forcing some food into her daughter was useless.

"My stomach's too upset … like Lightning's. Mind if I eat later, Mom?"

"That works for me," Cammi answered, pulling rain boots and rain gear from the mudroom. No matter what, Cammi willed herself she would remain positive throughout this newest emergency. One thing for certain, she and Jenna would be getting wet today.

Cammi went to the stairwell and called for Michael to wake up. "Get up honey, we need you down here."

The wind picked up. Heavy rain battered the windows, the noise from it drowned out the morning television show.

"Michael, please!" Impatient, she called again while stomping around in her boots and heavy rain jacket.

He appeared at the top of the landing, disheveled and angry, scratching at his ribs. "What the hell is going on here? And why do you suddenly need me?"

"Please, Michael," she begged, exasperated with his persistent short temper. "Jenna's horse is sick, and I need to get out to the barn to help her right now! Please call the school to excuse Jenna for the day. Also, I have not fed Renee her breakfast yet."

Renee slowly walked down the stairs, confused over the early morning commotion. She was rubbing the sleep from her eyes after having been awakened by the argument.

"Why me?" He was obviously unsympathetic and determined to be unreasonable. "Can't Renee get her own cereal? I'm tired and I'm going back to bed. Call me when this most recent calamity is over. Everything is such drama around here!"

Cammi prepared Renee a bowl of Rice Krispies with milk, and sat her down in front of the television to watch the morning cartoons.

"Honey," she said to Renee, "we are going out to walk Lightning for a short time. I'll call you from Mrs. Titus's house to see how you're doing, and I'll let you know how much better Lightning is feeling."

Renee nodded sleepily, crunching down on her first mouthful of cereal.

The worst of the storm had passed, so Cammi and Jenna were able to walk the horse up and down the Old Mill Road. They were careful to avoid the deep muddy puddles that had formed from the heavy rain. After twenty minutes, they stopped. However, Lightning was evidently still uncomfortable. Therefore, they began the routine again, walking up and down the road a second time.

At one point as they walked past the house, Cammi looked up and noticed Michael. He was in an upstairs window looking out and scowling at them. Puzzled, she could have sworn she saw someone standing behind him, but then realized it must have been an illusion from the wet windowpanes.

An hour later, dripping wet to the skin, they walked Lightning back into her stall, the pony seemingly feeling some small relief from her malady.

"Will you be all right?" Cammi asked Jenna, who pleaded to stay behind with her horse.

"I want you to promise to stay out of her box stall, because she may have some spasms and decide to roll," instructed Cammi. "Just water her. I'll go to the house and make you some warm soup, and then I want you to come home and put on some dry clothes before you come back here. Do I have a deal?"

"Sure, Mom. I'll be there in a few minutes."

But she wasn't, and after a half hour, Cammi reluctantly sent her scowling husband out to fetch Jenna and bring her home.

Cammi was in the kitchen when, without any forewarning, the front door flung open. Michael had kicked the door aside with his foot. He stepped into the living room with Jenna in his arms. Her limp wet body dripped large puddles of rainwater onto the floor.

Cammi screamed."What did you do to her? Oh my God, Michael, is she all right?"

"I didn't do it," he mumbled. "I swear to you, Cammi, I found her like this in the stall."

Cammi grabbed for Jenna and screamed again, but realized Jenna did not move. Cammi collapsed to the floor.

"You did it!" she cried, rocking the dead child in her arms. "You must have done it! You're a monster. I know you did it! You wouldn't help us! How could you do this to her?"

Cammi stroked Jenna's wet hair and felt a huge bump, and saw an open gash on her head. She noticed blood coming from the child's nose and mouth. She looked at her daughter's face and saw that her eyes were open and glazed, blind to her mother.

Cammi became incoherent. She rocked her daughter's body, overwhelmed and lost with shocked grief.

Some of the neighbors within proximity of the house became alarmed at the screams and gathered into the Fanelli kitchen in stunned silence. Cammi looked for Michael, but she did not see him among the many unrecognizable faces in the room. In a daze, Cammi saw Renee sitting on the sofa alone, sobbing. Moments later, the house filled with police officers and ambulance medics. Medical technicians carefully pried her hands free from the fierce grip she had on Jenna's limp body.

"Noooo, give her back to me!" she said, grasping at the empty air.

Suddenly, poor Jenna was whisked away from her arms. Cammi reached for Renee and held her to her breast, cognizant of the child's grief.

Several friends stayed the night to comfort Cammi and Renee. Friends sat around talking past midnight, whispering. Each one tried to determine where Michael could possibly have gone. Cammi, thankfully drugged by her doctor, was asleep in her bed, Renee near her side. In her hazy, drugged mind, Cammi dreamed of a misty white emptiness with fluffy pink and white clouds moving swiftly across a gray sky.

Confused and burdened with excruciating painful feelings of grief and guilt, Michael was feeling empty and numb as he steered his car away from the house. He drove mindlessly until a plan began to surface and take shape. He felt sure he did not hurt Jenna. He was positive he had found her already dead in the box stall.

But other thoughts invaded his confused mind. During a brief cognizant moment, he wondered where these feelings originated. He sensed these images had emerged from a seldom used area of his cerebral gray matter. What came to mind was a plain and simple solution to his dilemma and solved all his immediate problems. He gave little thought to his dead daughter Jenna, or Cammi and Renee, or the aftermath.

He knew that this solution was the only path open to him. Astonishingly in anticipation of the end, he felt at once giddy and lightheaded. His destiny was close at hand. An unseen hand lifted every burden from his soul.

He parked on the railroad tracks and waited for the train to arrive. An overwhelming sense of peace washed over him the instant he heard the train whistle. As if in slow motion, he glanced over to look at the old abandoned store decorated with Christmas lights. In the millisecond before the train demolished Michael and the car he realized in muddled confusion that it wasn't Christmastime at all and Jeb's store had been closed for thirty some odd years.

About this time, Renee awakened to the sounds of pots and dishes clattering about in the kitchen below. Phantom scratching noises emanated from the walls. She lay in bed terrified and frozen. Hideous ghostly musical high-pitched children's laughter filled the room. She lay in bed alongside her drugged and unconscious mother, her eyes rolling left and right, wide with terror searching for the source of the haunting sounds she alone could hear.

# Benny Treadwell and Clara

──────────── ▼ ────────────

Mrs. Treadwell's health swiftly declined. She had suffered a second stroke that paralyzed her left side. Her speech was impaired, but she could still cause a ruckus among her nursing staff.

At one point Mrs. Bailey, one of her nurses, declared herself unwanted and unwelcome in the household. "Even those blasted ghosts don't want me here, Mr. Treadwell. I beg that you release me from my contract. That mother of yours is a hateful old woman. She clings to that Bible of hers, yet treats me as though I am dirt under her feet. She is ungrateful, and she has directed me to leave."

She pulled her hair aside and displayed bruises around the temple and fore-head. "You must realize, sir, this happened because I tried to snatch that book from her grasp to wash her hands. I must say she has lost no strength in her right hand. Smacked me in the head she did with the book, and beat me about the body."

One icy cold day, Nurse Tierney ran outdoors barefoot into the snowdrifts. She said the ghosts terrified her. She walked home shoeless, swearing that she would never set foot into the Treadwell house again. She deemed it unholy and haunted.

Gossip about the house being haunted spread through the community. The neighbors that had occasionally stopped by to see Mrs. Treadwell were too frightened to visit any longer. Benny knew the only way he could find reliable help would be through advertising in the surrounding area newspapers.

A surprising break came the following month when a packet arrived in the mail. The return address was from Herkimer County. A young woman cited excellent qualifications, and requested an interview for permanent nursing position. She wrote that she had been born in Cortland and for several years worked in a local hospital. Benny thought that maybe she was seeking this position because it would transport her out of the area. She claimed to be an adventuresome spirit. Her name was Clara Edison.

Expecting an older woman, Benny attempted to conceal his surprise when Clara arrived at the appointed interview time. She was the most attractive woman he had seen since his trip to New York City some years back. Her long legs and willowy figure made her appear taller than she actually was. Her blonde hair was cut into the new bob that personified the late twenties look and her cute smile made Benny melt.

This is it. Mother could not refuse such a cheerful young woman.

Clara appeared energized even when relaxed. During conversation she remained in constant motion. She fidgeted throughout the interview, pushing her long bangs aside, inspecting her manicured nails, and smoothing her skirt over her knees.

Benny could not keep his eyes off her. She wore silk stockings that no other woman wore in this part of the country. Her sleek long black skirt with ruffled hem seemed too feminine and somewhat out of place for this part of the state.

He knew she had the job long before the interview was over; on the contrary, he was uneasy that she might refuse the job offer.

"Miss Edison, any relation to Thomas?"

"Everyone asks me that, and the answer is no. We are possibly distant cousins."

"Tell me about your hospital training." He pretended to listen, but was really thinking about how cute she looked when she spoke. He also was entranced by the constant, deliberate motion of her body.

"Fact is Mr. Treadwell; I have references from past patients, and a doctor's letter of recommendation. I came here today prepared to stay. I will give you two days trial employment to see if your mother approves of me."

She better approve, Benny thought, suddenly tired of all the older companions he had tried to match up with his mother's stubborn personality.

"Well, if you're prepared to stay, let me show you to your room." He brought Clara to Aunt Geraldine's refurbished quarters but quickly changed his mind.

"On second thought we have some spare bedrooms upstairs that should meet with your approval. How about the one closest to my mother's room."

"Sounds like a perfect situation, sir."

"Please call me Benny. Everyone does."

"Not Benjamin?"

"No, that was my father's name. I grew up being called Benny and feel most comfortable with it, Clara."

He liked the sound of her name.

As they passed the fireplace, Clara ran her hands along the mahogany carved mantel. "You have a beautiful home here, Benny."

They climbed the stairs and peeked into Mother's room.

"We'll let her sleep for now, there is plenty of time to meet her," Benny said, hoping that when his mother awakened she would be easier to manage and so more of a pleasant nature, during her initial interview with Clara.

To his amazement, his mother fell in love with Clara, and before long, Benny did too. Clara spoke to everyone in a kind and unassuming manner, and her tone held an edge of humor. She was an uncommonly beautiful person.

Clara started right out entertaining her charge. She told Benny's mother the story about the murder of Grace Brown, and the subsequent famous trial and conviction of Chester Gillette in Herkimer County. Clara taught the older woman to sing the "Ballad of Big Moose Lake" in an attempt to exercise her weak vocal cords.

One afternoon Clara came downstairs to speak with Benny who was relaxing on the porch.

"So, who are the children whose spirits are trapped in this house?" she asked directly.

"How do you know about that?" he asked, surprised at her question.

"At first, I distinctly heard them giggling, then I saw them playing in the back-yard. In a vision, I saw pink ribbons blowing in the wind above their heads. They turned to face me and pointed in my direction. Haven't you ever had this vision?"

"I wish I could see them again. Are you in tune with any other paranormal visions in this house?"

"Yes, there is a very nasty woman in the kitchen."

"How can you know this all so quickly?"

Clara folded her hands in her lap. "When I was young, Grace Brown was missing, and mind you, this was before anyone even knew she was dead. Everyone in the Adirondack's was searching for her, and one night I had a strange dream. It was a dream about a baby crying uncontrollably." She paused. "The next day I told my mother about it, and sure enough, Grace Brown was found murdered that day. Two years later, I had the same dream, and one day later my father died."

"Oh, I'm so sorry." He took her hand and squeezed.

"Thank you. At any rate, it has happened half a dozen times since then. I have now decided I am in tune with the supernatural spirit world."

Benny took a deep breath. "Is there anything here that truly frightens you?"

"Yes, that horrible woman in the kitchen is mean spirited and could conceivably cause harm to anyone who is susceptible to that sort of thing."

"She already has," Benny answered calmly.

"I won't ask more if you don't want to tell me."

"Maybe it's best that you know."

Benny told her about how Floyd had died, but he did not reveal the fact that Aunt Geraldine had murdered Minnie. He was still too sensitive about that information and worried that Catherine would find out the truth.

"What has made you continue to live here with all the ghostly activity and horrible memories?" she asked.

He had to think for a few moments before he could answer. "It wasn't until recently that I was even aware of all the ghostly haunting here. I realize you might find it hard to believe, but it only started to spook me after my father told me about some of the incidents that terrified him."

"You must live in your own little world."

"I admit not ever really believing in ghosts and goblins, but I'm in the process of reviewing my beliefs."

She laughed, shaking her head at him.

"I have actually planned to move from here as soon as Mother is stable enough to leave."

"Where do you plan to move to?"

"I'm building a large house in Lake Placid."

"I'd love to see it one day," she said.

"I'm sure you will. First, I would like it if you could meet my sister Catherine and her husband William. They have a child who is eight months old now."

"I couldn't understand, but now I realize," she said. "Catherine won't come here to visit her mother because she is frightened of the ghosts, right?"

"And there are too many horrible memories for her here."

"People are usually terrified of things they cannot explain."

"You do put that well."

Exactly one month to the day, Clara dreamed about a baby crying uncontrollably. She awoke with an unshakable feeling of unutterable terror.

# Benny Treadwell and Mother

―――――――――― ▼ ――――――――――

Upon awakening from her prophetic dream, Clara rushed to Mrs. Treadwell's room to check on her. Thankfully, she was still peacefully asleep. With a sigh of relief, she put on her robe and joined Benny downstairs for morning coffee.

"I dreamed about a baby crying last night. I have already checked to make sure your mother is safe."

"Well, that's excellent news to hear Mother is safe." He reached for her hand. "You know I've been awake since five this morning thinking about you. I think it's time I let you know that I care a great deal for you and don't know what I would do without you here beside me."

Clara rose from her chair to sit beside him. She kissed him softly on the lips.

"I am aware of that and I want you to know the feelings are mutual."

Before either of them could say more, a loud rumble rolled through the house. The room seemed to take on a life of its own. The walls and floor began to shake slowly. The couple looked around for the source of the commotion. The rumbling became increasingly more intense. Suddenly, the hot coffee in their cups began to boil and overflow. Crockery rattled in the pantry, and at random, dishes seemed tossed full force from the shelves by unseen hands. Loud knocking noises emanated from the walls.

Clara screamed and shielded herself with her hands as ceramic and glassware hurled in her direction. She was immediately cut on the head and around her face. Benny sought to protect her, but he too was plummeted by glassware, pots, and pans. The serving platters and cups became dangerous projectiles spinning around them, cutting and ripping at their bodies. Knives and forks streaked through the air as though an unseen archer had targeted them, striking bull's eye, and lodging in their arms and into the walls.

The rumbling noises reached a deafening pitch. Benny imagined the two of them were in a tornado—a powerful, howling wind engulfed them.

He grabbed Clara's hand and dragged her to him. He scooped her up and half carrying her, he ran to the kitchen to escape the onslaught. The minute they stepped over the threshold of the breakfast room, there was an abrupt halt to the diabolical attack. They looked around disbelieving the magnitude of destruction.

"Mother!" Benny screamed. He raced furiously upstairs, taking two steps at a time, Clara at his heels.

The sight inside his mother's room resembled the breakfast room. Everything ripped from the walls, and anything movable thrown at his mother while she lay upon her bed. Her pillows contained glass shards protruding from the down stuffing, the result of picture frames and photos hurled in her direction.

His mother had somehow managed to crawl onto the floor. She died after dragging her partially paralyzed and bloodied body toward her sacred Bible hanging from the opposite wall. The Bible had been pierced by a glass shard that held it in place just beyond her reach.

Shocked, Benny and Clara sank to their knees beside his mother's body. Benny cradled her head in his arms and searched for signs of life, but he knew she was dead; her eyes wide open in terror from the wild attack.

After calling the church rectory, the doctor, and the police department, Benny and Clara sat outside trying to decide what to do next. Dr. Merk made the decision for them. He transported them to his office where he stitched their wounds, and then drove them to his home.

"You need to rest, and then we can talk about what possibly could have precipitated this ungodly attack on your family today," the doctor said. "At the crack of dawn tomorrow I have arranged to meet with some workers who have volunteered to clean up your home. I have also settled arrangements at the mortuary for your mother. I think it's best if you both stayed here with us tonight, and through tomorrow at the very least."

Benny and Clara nodded. They were not in any condition to make decisions.

Joe was in charge of the workers who cautiously entered the Treadwell home the next morning. The workers packed some of Clara and Benny's personal belongings. It took a full day to clean up the gory mess. At the end of the day, Joe visited Benny at Dr. Merk's home, and provided him with a full assessment of the damages.

"I have to admit," Joe began, "I only stayed in the house as short a time as was necessary, but I had this feeling that whatever haunts that place was gathering strength. It put me into some sort of hypnotic state that unexpectedly lulled me into a false sense of security."

He reported that all of the kitchen dishes and glasses were lost, and the men discovered numerous utensils stuck in the wainscoting attesting to the fury of the attack.

"It was a pity having to clean your mother's bloody room, and I admit it caused me distress to linger in there any longer than needed."

Joe opened a leather case and handed the contents to Benny. With his voice barely above a whisper, he said, "I removed the glass shard that held your mother's Bible to the wall. Have to admit, I thumbed through it and it sent chills up my spine. I think you'll need some private time alone to read this."

With that, he departed. Benny opened the old Bible. Some letters along with an old photo fell onto the floor. He and Clara examined the photo of a strange young man dressed in aviator leather with goggles propped on top of his head. He sat upon a motorbike with a sidecar. On the back of the photo written in pencil was the date 1910.

Clara read the first letter then handed it to Benny.

*Darling,*
*You have been in my thoughts the whole of last night and today. It has been so wonderful, our meeting as we did. I patiently wait to hear from you the date of our next rendezvous.*
*Obsessively in love, Robert*

*Dearest Robert,*
*How wonderful it was to spend the entire afternoon in your arms. For me it was a dream come true. I don't know how I existed so long without your love.*
*Forever, Elizabeth*

*My darling Elizabeth,*

*The need to see you all the time tortures me, and I send this post to convince you that we need to arrange for you to be with me always. You cannot endure the loveless marriage you are trapped in. I understand your argument about your obligations, but in this life there is only love. Mine! My love is real and endless!*

*You are my obsession, Robert*

One letter was returned from Brasher Falls that was sent to the Mill office.

*Darling,*

*He knows. He has found and destroyed some of your lovely letters, and he appears homicidal. Such uncontrolled anger I have never witnessed before in any human being. Please do not come here, it is too dangerous. I hope this post reaches you before you leave. I am unable to reach you in any other fashion and am frantically anxious for.*

*I will love you always, I fear for your life, Elizabeth*

"Benny, this is probably the motorbike that was found in the lake," Clara said, pointing to the photo.

Benny dropped the letter in dazed submission. He nodded slowly, unable to speak. His eyes held the shock from yesterday compounded a hundred times over.

"Please," he begged Clara. "We must get as far away from that godforsaken house as soon as possible."

Benny and Clara spent another few days at the Merk residence recovering from the shock of the past days.

"Maybe we should go to Malone, to Catherine's house, until the house in Lake Placid is completed. We can leave here after your mother's funeral tomorrow. Maybe stay at the Inn at Gabriel's," Clara suggested.

"Let's go for a walk into the woods where I can think," Benny said.

They did not speak as they hiked along a marked trail.

Benny broke the silence. "Knowing what we know, I cannot in good conscious sell the property to an innocent family. Who would ever believe the enormous strength of the evil powers that reside there? I know how dangerously haunted it is now. My mother died from a heinous supernatural attack, and I don't know how to fight the forces of darkness. This has been an invasion of our personal reality."

After some minutes mulling over the last day's horror, he said, "I now know my father murdered that Robert person. So, in effect, my mother and father were inadvertently responsible for the accident that killed Floyd."

The two reached a pass where the trail forked. They chose the one that led to a lake.

"I feel like I've lived in a household of murderers," Benny said. "I must take that into account in any decisions I make about the transfer of the property. I know not one person in this area who will even touch the property ... not after the horror has taken place."

He stopped and gathered Clara in his arms.

"I need to come up with a viable solution. Then I can operate my business and make arrangements for sale of the mill. If I have learned one thing from this demonic attack, it is that I want to spend the rest of my life with you in another place, a safe house."

"I'm sorry your mother was so brutally attacked and killed."

"I don't know what to feel about that, but now I know why she guarded that Bible of hers with such fervor. You know, a long time ago, I overheard my mother and father arguing. At that time, I was hiding in my tree fort with Floyd. We never quite understood what they were talking about until I read those letters today. Now everything falls into place. I suddenly understand the accusations from that argument."

"Finding out all of this at once must be terrible for you."

"Not really, I hid behind my stupidity refusing to see what was staring at me all along. I should have seen it coming. And my father warned me, warned me about the forces of evil that surround the house. But never in my wildest dreams could I fathom such a horrific attack."

"I would never have believed that evil spirits could physically attack with such strength," Clara said.

The funeral for Elizabeth Mary Morgan was the next day. The church over-flowed with mourners who showed up because they had heard about the mysterious circumstances that surrounded her death. Hushed tones from the congregation were heard during Mass. Catherine and William were thankfully able to attend. Catherine displayed signs of deep mourning, her eyes swollen and red. Her shoulders heaved deeply as she sobbed under the weight of this latest tragedy. Finally, the family escorted the coffin to the adjacent cemetery, the Treadwell plot readied to receive the latest victim from a terrifying death.

After the funeral service had concluded, Benny went to his sister. He tried to explain to her the circumstances from that tragic morning, but she refused to listen. She held her hands over her ears. "The least I know of the circumstances that killed Mother, the better I can sleep at night. I cannot continue to relive these abominable tragedies."

William waited alongside the car for Catherine, who was still speaking with her brother.

"I am going to arrange for a priest or an exorcist to cleanse and bless the house before we sell it. I can't imagine another family suffering as we have. It would be inhumane not to inform them up front about the tragedies we have suffered," Benny said.

Catherine agreed with that idea.

Before William and Catherine took leave to return to Malone, Benny took his brother-in-law aside. "I need your help in disposing of the property," he said. "I cannot sell this place to just anyone. I cannot bear the thought of another family suffering as we have. The place reeks of death and murderous deeds."

"So?" William asked.

"I have a job for you. It's just an idea, but only you can make it happen. You're the only man I know with direct contact to murderers and thieves," Benny said in jest, referring to William's profession as a defense attorney.

William appeared puzzled at first, but as Benny outlined his plan to dispose of the house and property, William's smile grew wider. "Only you, brother-in-law, can devise a scheme so perfectly appropriate. I'll get on it tomorrow. I promise I won't let you down."

Before he got into his car to return to Malone, William turned to Benny. "I already have two fellows in mind who would be perfect caretakers for your home. Meanwhile, we'll have to see what Catherine really meant by having the house blessed by a clergyman. I will have to arrange to carry out her wishes before we can proceed."

Benny stood alongside the driver's side of the car as William prepared to drive off, he ended the conversation on a happier note, "Clara and I are planning to be married by Thanksgiving. We plan to keep it small and private."

Catherine finally smiled. Benny got behind the wheel of his car and then each one drove away in opposite directions from the cemetery at dusk.

# BENNY TREADWELL
# FATHER FLANNERY

▼

Father Flannery arrived earlier than the appointed time, so he remained seated in his car with the heater full blast waiting for Reverend Glass to arrive with the homeowner. The temperature had plummeted sharply the night before. He blew his runny nose and coughed out the last remnants of a nasty cold that had prevented him from driving up from Glens Falls last month.

He carefully surveyed the area and noticed children playing in the snow-covered backyard. It took a few moments for it to register, but he realized the children had no overcoats on. They ran and chased one another but left no footprints in the snow.

He blinked and when he looked, the children were gone.

*Probably a figment of my vivid imagination.*

He turned to study the house, which appeared benign. It had white gingerbread trim on the roof peaks, and the clapboard siding was painted a new mustard yellow. He was told no one lived in the house any longer, so was surprised to see curtains move in an upstairs window and a woman's face appear. She stared at him for a moment then slowly drew the curtain closed.

He felt his skin prickle under his heavy woolen coat, and he plunged his hands into the wide pockets. He wrapped his coat tighter around his body. An unwelcome image sprang into his memory from the first time he had performed the rite of exorcism, and had come face to face with Satan and the powers of demons. He recalled the ferocious battle that ensued, a battle he had come close to losing. He coughed into his closed fist, hacking until he was able to loosen the tightness that had formed in his chest.

A car pulled up behind his. He recognized his old friend John Glass, minister of the Episcopal Church. They had been close buddies as children, John entering the Episcopal ministry and he entering the Catholic seminary.

"Hope you haven't been waiting long," John said.

"Let me introduce you to the owner of the house, Benjamin Treadwell, and his brother-in-law William Tyler, attorney at law from Malone."

They shook hands. The men appeared uneasy and shifted from one foot to another.

"It's freezing outside here, let's at least go into the house," Benny said, breaking the tension.

"I thought you told me the house was vacant," queried Father Flannery.

"It is," Benny said.

"I could have sworn I saw a woman in the window upstairs."

"You probably did see someone."

Father Flannery shivered.

"The house is vacant of live persons," said Benny. "There have been many recent sightings by my neighbors; faces appearing in the window upstairs, and small children playing outside."

Father Flannery blanched at this. He feared this demonic encounter would be as bad as the first time. The men settled into the large sofa and chairs in the living room while Benny lit a fire in the fireplace. The flames did nothing to warm the frigid air. They sat and talked, their frozen breath filling the room while Benny outlined the past tragedies and the final attack. A sudden creaking in the rafters drew their attention to the ceiling, the sound of footsteps upstairs.

Father Flannery quickly unclasped a small case. He removed a purple vestment and stole, and draped it over his heavy overcoat. He immediately began sprinkling holy water. He held a crucifix erect as he began to mouth prayers. All at once, an alien presence of evil engulfed the men. Father Flannery doubled over in a coughing fit before he readjusted his vestment, and then he bravely proceeded to walk through each icy cold room with the three men close behind.

"Our Father who art in heaven hallowed be thy name. Thy kingdom come."

Loud banging inside the walls echoed through the rooms interrupting the sacred prayers. A distinct heartbeat rose ever louder. In unison, the men began to repeat the Lord's Prayer. Benny, William, and John stayed huddled and as close as possible to the priest.

Slowly they began to climb the stairs. "Depart, then, impious one, depart, accursed one, depart with all your deceits, for God has willed that man should be his temple. Why do you linger here?" Father Flannery recited aloud.

The noises reached a deafening pitch, and then suddenly a horrific green creature appeared at the top of the stairs and lunged at Father Flannery. The priest fell to his knees on the steps, coughing and holding his chest, the gold crucifix raised above his head with one hand.

"Your place is in solitude; your abode is in the nest of serpents; get down and crawl with them," he continued.

He coughed uncontrollably. The creature attacked him ferociously with claws and fangs. The other men cowered on the landing below.

"It is he who expels you. He who casts you out. From whose sight nothing is hidden. It is he who repels you ..." Father Flannery spoke in a low, croaked whisper gasping for air.

Benny, although shocked and terrified, helped the priest to his feet and supported his limp body. Suddenly tornado strength winds engulfed them. Voices of long gone, dead demons shrieked atrocities in their direction.

"Therefore, I adjure you every unclean spirit, every specter from hell, every satanic power, in the name of Jesus," the priest croaked.

Something supernatural lifted his body and flung him down the stairs. Father Flannery tumbled headfirst and crashed into the men huddled on the landing below.

The men stared at the priest flailing his arms and legs, the crucifix ripped from his grasp. Benny attempted to raise the priest to a sitting position. Father Flannery opened his crazed eyes as flames shot from them. Thick green vomit poured from his mouth and onto his vestments.

Benny grabbed hold of the crucifix, curled the priest's fingers around it, and slammed it against his body. A sizzling arose, and the men smelled burning flesh. The priest screamed in agony. Suddenly the fire disappeared from his eyes, and his head flopped onto one shoulder.

Knocking sounds began again, louder than before. Hundreds of transparent ghostly forms with skeletal faces dove at them filling the stairwell with horrific indistinguishable images and sounds.

Each man struggled to drag Father Flannery from the stairwell into the living room, the crucifix still smoldering on his chest. He was incoherent, thrashing his extremities and rolling his head from side to side.

They carried him from the house and lay him on top of William's woolen coat spread upon the stone steps. It took several moments until the priest stopped convulsing, and only then did Benny breathe a sigh of relief.

"I had no idea the haunting was as bad as that," John said, stroking the hair on Father Flannery's head. The priest slowly regained consciousness. He moaned and coughed up green phlegm.

"Since that fateful morning when Clara, Mother, and I were attacked, this evil presence seems to be gaining strength," Benny said. He turned to William. "I guess short of burning down the house, we need to come up with some sort of a plan."

"You can't possibly mean that you would allow some innocent bystander to purchase this house from you," John said.

"No, absolutely not!" cried Benny. "William and I have devised a plan that now, under the circumstances of that terrible day's grisly assault, may be our only way out!"

Benny ran into the house to retrieve some blankets for the priest. They bundled the semiconscious man into them and carried him to his car. Within several minutes, they arrived at the Episcopal Church rectory where they put him in bed.

Benny phoned Dr. Merk. "I know he has been sick this last month, I hope this doesn't worsen his condition." His voice shook as he spoke to the doctor.

But his condition did worsen. Father Flannery caught a raging case of pneumonia, and died twenty days later in a hospital; his friend John gave him last rites. The two old friends had held hands and recited the Lord's Prayer before Father Flannery drew his last breath.

# Benny's Solution

▼

Benny shook Calvin's limp, arthritic hand and studied him. His skin hung loose and leathery around his dirty neckline, scorched brown by countless years laying in the sun-filled jail yard in Dannemora. Whatever few teeth remained were a sickening brown color, stained by nicotine from endless cigarettes. His breath reeked. Yet, Calvin smiled. An ugly smirk made his wet watery eyes glisten in the light. They were hungry eyes, hungry to possess everything owned by anyone else. He sat on the front steps, pretending to appear personable, continually eyeing the house with an expression of ravenous greed and pompous pretentiousness.

If he were an animal, he would soon be foaming at the mouth.

"I believe your lawyer, William Tyler, has outlined our agreement," Benny began.

"He sure did, right after my release," Calvin answered.

Uncomfortable, Calvin shuffled his weight from one side to another. In a feeble attempt to hide his overall confusion, he crossed his legs and hoped it conveyed to Benny that he was in complete control of this unusual situation.

That lawyer had explained things just fine, Calvin thought with glee.

In painstaking detail, William had explained the conditions of the real estate contract and of the haunting. In an effort to fully disclose everything, he had minutely described some of the past events that had transpired. The selling point for Calvin was that he could live in the house for five years, and then he would own it lock, stock, and barrel. Never mind the otherworldly guests; he figured he would deal with them if they ever showed up.

Nobody in his or her right mind would ever have considered presenting such a deal to a convict. And, no convict could ever dream of owning a huge house, furnishings included. Calvin imagined it to be a mansion, and he was determined that one day it would be his. Besides, he knew that even if he went away for a spell, what with Benny and his wife living in Lake Placid, they would never even know he had left.

"He explained to you the five-year rule?" Benny asked.

"Yes, sir."

"You understand that the contract is null and void if the five-year rule is not met?"

"Yes, sir." Calvin spit a dark brown slime into the steps that made a long drip down to the step below.

"Then let me show you around," Benny said, feeling his stomach tumble and twist.

They entered the house, and Calvin was at once overwhelmed. His eyes darted around in birdlike fashion taking in the grand surroundings. There were things he dared only dream about during his difficult early life and subsequent confinement.

"You really want *me* to live here, surrounded by this much luxury?" Calvin began. "It's a steal with only a couple of spooky ghosts to deal with. What other tricks are you hiding up your sleeve, Captain?"

Calvin appeared to swoon and fell backward into an easy chair.

"And who did *you* kill to get this rich?" Calvin smiled, a sickening grin framed by the deep gouges in his face.

"Mr. Haige, I did not kill and I did not steal, speak only for yourself!" Benny swallowed hard the bile that involuntarily rose in his throat. "Look, I need to make this perfectly clear. This is a business arrangement. I will pay you two thousand dollars per year, and if you stay for the mandated term of five years, I will sign the house over to you with no money exchanged. That I believe were the terms spelled out to you by your lawyer."

Benny was fully informed that Calvin had been convicted of two murder charges, and that he had been recently released after serving close to twenty years.

"I do want to keep the surrounding land in my family's name. Are you prepared to sign this agreement, Mr. Haige?" Benny sat down in a chair opposite Calvin.

"Sure, Captain. By the looks of things, you need to skip town and want me, your piddling caretaker, to shoulder the brunt of caring for your maliciously haunted sweet abode." His lungs whistled in a deep breath. "Now, I know you're gonna lay low somewhere far away from the chains clanking in the night. But what about me?"

"Calvin, do you agree or not?" Benny was becoming exasperated and quickly losing patience with the likes of a kind of person he had never dealt with before. His foot began tapping, impatient for an answer.

"Do you mean I have no right to ask any questions, Captain?"

"Sure you do," Benny said, feeling uneasy about spilling his guts to this stranger. He sank deeper into the chair. "I was born in this house. My father ran a successful business from here. I have buried everyone, well, almost everyone except my sister."

He chose his words carefully reluctant to reveal too much personal information.

"I got married last year, and my wife and I have a home in Lake Placid. We plan to stay there. We no longer want to live in this house. I only hope to keep the land for sentimental value."

He looked Calvin in the eye. "Besides, my wife is frightened, terrified of ghosts. Does that answer your questions, Mr. Haige?"

"Are you some sort of liberal do-gooder," he said with a wide grin, "who plans to rehabilitate me and turn me into some kind of person who would never have committed a gruesome murder?"

"No, I'm none of that; I am a man trying to do what's best. This house has been witness to murder before, so it will not be unusual for you to call it home one day."

Benny smirked. The palms of his hands began to sweat. He casually wiped them on his pants. Calvin stared at him for a moment and then grinned. He knew he had Benny going now.

"Skeletons in your closet, Captain?" He began to prod Benny. "Betcha' most likely they've been hidden away for years. Are you scared of bringing shame down on your family tree, eh?"

Calvin raised his brows; his intense eyes scanned Benny's facial expression for the smallest sign of weakness.

"There is very little that scares me anymore, you evil wimp of a man. I understand you killed a child and a woman, the woman being your wife. You only got away with a light sentence because she was in bed with another man, and the child happened to be in the way of your car during your pitiful escape."

Losing all sense of reason, Benny leaped out of the chair and grabbed Calvin by the throat. With a horrific pounding in his head, Benny suddenly realized he had better lighten the death grip, because the color of the hideous man's face quickly changed to a bright red, and his tongue hung from his gaping mouth. Slowly, ever so slowly, Benny released his strangling grip, but kept his knee tight on Calvin's torso, pinning the small squirming man to the floor.

"Take my offer or leave it, buddy," Benny finally said, shaken by his own aggressive and unusual reaction.

Benny surmised the house had affected him more than he had realized or could have believed. He knew only one thing stopped him from killing Calvin. It was the recognition of fear in the vile man's eyes when he could no longer breathe. Benny let loose of his knee on Calvin's torso and stood up. He held out his hand to assist Calvin to his feet, and Benny glimpsed a slight bit of appreciation when Calvin tipped his head in his direction.

"Look, I don't need to love you; I'll save that for my wife," Benny said half-apologetically.

Calvin massaged his neck, red finger marks brightly visible on his skin. He doubled over in a spasm of heavy gurgling and coughed. Finally, unceremoniously, he spit onto the oak floor.

"You've got a deal, mate," he said. He walked to the table and signed the contract.

When Benny left, he felt a twinge of pity for the strange man. His only concession was that Calvin fully understood the terrible happenings that had taken place in the house over the years. There was also the possibility that Calvin would never detect or have any sensation of fear while living in the house. Benny had learned firsthand how the surroundings could lull one into a false sense of comfort, blinding one from the knowledge that demons shared your abode. He was comfortable too, that Calvin had no friends, or family who could possibly be in any danger, and he knew the man would somehow find delight living in the pure luxury of the house.

Gratefully, it would bide him and Clara some needed time to make a decision whether or not to raze the house. He could never understand his stubborn reluctance to destroy the structure. He imagined it had to do with his feelings that his father had built it. Even though he now understood that evil forces occupied the house, he had lived immersed in it for so many years, he found he had finally accepted it as his plight.

Benny walked outside and got into his car. Before he pulled out of the driveway, he took a last look at the house. He gasped, because unexpectedly, he saw the lights go on in an upstairs window. A dark figure of a woman appeared, her face firmly pressed against the window. She watched him for a minute and then slowly and deliberately she drew the curtains closed. Benny knew in his heart that she would patiently wait for his return, remaining trapped in that heinous place forever.

He drove slowly down the street watching the house disappear in the rearview mirror. He imagined he heard its familiar heartbeat even from this distance.

# THE GRAVEYARD

▼

"I don't want to go back to that scary old house," Renee sobbed.

"You can stay here with Grandma and Grandpa while I go. It's been a full year, Renee. A year since ... since ... the accident. I have also felt safe living here, but I have to go back to get the house ready to sell."

Renee crawled into her mother's lap and snuggled into a fetal position. She sucked her thumb, a habit she had picked up only recently. Cammi smoothed the soft curls on Renee's head and gently tucked one curl around her exposed ear. She felt tremendous compassion for her daughter. Renee had not only lost her father, but she also lost her sister. Jenna had been her very best friend in the whole world.

"If I go with you, can I sleep at Mrs. Titus's house instead of our old house?" Renee dared to ask.

"Of course, if that makes you feel safer we can stay there together and only go back to that scary old house for a couple of hours during the day. I want to pack up our family photos and personal belongings. Then I'll call the realtor and we'll be finished. Then sweetheart, we can be in Florida before the first day of school begins. Also," she remembered, "don't forget that Grandma and Grandpa go down to Fort Myers to stay in their condo in January, and we can all be together again then."

"Can we stop at special places that we went to before like Fort Ticonderoga and Ausable Chasm?" She wiped the tears from her eyes with her pink pajama sleeve. "Can we can take a raft down the river again? Remember when Daddy took us, and we had so much fun that day. I remember me and Jenna giggling and getting all wet and stuff."

Renee's lower lip quivered, but she held back from crying. Cammi thought she was getting better at controlling her tears after this long difficult year.

Cammi was fully aware that she too had to gather up whatever remnants of courage that remained within her to face the inevitable pain of going back to the Old Mill Road. Back to face the excruciating memories stored in the walls of that old house.

"I'll telephone Mrs. Titus later today and see when it would be a good time for her to have us as her house guests."

Mother and daughter sat on the bed lost in their memories, memories filled with happiness and memories filled with pain.

"Cammi," it was her father calling from the other room. "Mrs. Titus is on the phone for you."

*Must be telepathic.*

"How are you?" Mrs. Titus asked Cammi.

"Better now that I hear your voice. I was planning to call you later today. Renee and I are thinking about driving up to the area in a few weeks. We're planning to pack up some of our personal stuff at the house. We're finally able to move on and sell the old place. I've arranged to relocate to Fort Myers, Florida. My parents have a condo there, and Renee and I are looking forward to a complete lifestyle change."

"Funny, I had thought about that recently. I know it's been more than a year since you brought Jenna and Michael back to Long Island for burial. I thought the timing would be right now for you and Renee to come back. I've spoken to Benny and Clara recently, and they asked me about how you have fared this last year."

"Have they decided to meet with me?" Cammi asked excitedly.

"No, Clara is insistent about not stirring up any painful memories for Benny. She said once they walked away from their old house they never talked about it again. Now that he's an old man, he gets very emotional about what went on there. She is very protective of her husband."

"I had hoped they would reconsider and meet with me, even a telephone call would do. You did explain to them that I have some questions I need answered. Questions only they can answer about what went on in the house before we bought it."

"You know, Cammi, I already told you all I know."

"But there is more, Mrs. Titus. I don't mean to belittle what history you gave me. I've learned more about that place than I care to know, but there are some questions only Benny can answer. Some things I need to get straight in my own mind. I don't think I can fully recover from the horror of this last year without answers to my questions."

"I'll surely ask again for you, but it's like beating a dead horse to get her to budge. What is it you need to know? Maybe I can find out for you."

Cammi paused. How could she explain to Mrs. Titus that she needed to know if possibly, some hideous demonic specter drove Michael to his grave? She needed to talk about Benjamin Senior, about how he died, and why Michael had exhibited such a personality change after moving into the house. She needed to make sense of her confused suppositions. The whole experience was a jumbled mess of possibilities, all of which made little or no sense to her.

"It's so hard for me to explain to you," Cammi said. "I know you're looking out for my best interests, and I can accept Benny and Clara do not want to meet with me, but hopefully they'll have a change of heart when we get there."

"Clara is a stubborn old woman, not unlike me. I have never seen her waver from her convictions, but you never know. When do you think you'll be coming up this way?"

"As soon as you'll have us."

"Make your plans, dear. Most of the old timers around here have gone and died. Buried them all including my husband and daughter. And I don't have many people stop by anymore. Thank goodness for the little gossip with my neighbors over the fence. Ordinarily, it's just me and old Queenie, and of course, Mitzi my cat." She paused. "It would truly make an old lady happy to see both you and little Renee again."

"Has Calvin ever stopped by to see you since I've been gone?" Cammi inquired. "I remember a long time ago when we first bought the house, Calvin mentioned that he had dug up the old vehicle that Benjamin Senior was killed in. He said he found the old man's shoe still lodged inside the wreck. It was kind of an eerie thing, and I was wondering exactly where the vehicle was buried on the property. Thought that Calvin might still be hanging around there."

"That horrible man!" Mrs. Titus made a disagreeable sound.

"Hope to never see the likes of him again. I never could figure out why Benny allowed that man to live in his ancestral home. It is a desecration of the Treadwell family name. But in answer to your question, yes I have seen Calvin recently."

Mrs. Titus remembered the day well. "He did make hunting season last year with those ignorant sons of his, and he asked all kinds of things about what I thought you might end up doing with the house. I think he wanted it back. He probably would have foreclosed on you. I don't think that man has an ounce of honor in his body."

"The only good thing was that Michael had enough insurance money to pay off the old geezer," Cammi said.

"As for me, I don't remember anything about where the vehicle is buried. Come to think of it, it was Benny's old car, the one he brought home with him after the service. The same one his daddy got killed in."

"All right, Mrs. Titus, I will see you in a couple of weeks. I plan to get my car serviced so we can make the long drive safely. Renee is a little afraid, but I think it's something we both have to do in order to reconcile with the grief we are experiencing."

Cammi and Renee made several stops along the way. They picnicked along the bank of Taylor Pond and stopped to pick up groceries at the old Grand Union in Saranac Lake. As they drove past the church cemetery, Cammi applied the brakes and turned around in a driveway just past the cemetery. Something sparked her memory. She remembered what Marie had told her when she and Ron had visited last year. Today, Cammi had to see it for herself. She slowly drove through the maze of tombstones, Renee still asleep in the back seat of the car.

She came upon the Treadwell plot, separated from other gravestones by a short fence. The large monument towered above all the other tombstones.

She got out of the car and opened the creaky wrought iron gate that enclosed the family graves. She ran her hand along Benjamin Treadwell's ornately engraved tombstone. Touching it made the Treadwell family feel alive and real. Cammi imagined she felt an electrical charge emit in the palm of her hand.

She noted the inscription, the same as Marie had written down. *Benjamin Treadwell son of Malcolm and Mildred Treadwell.*

Cammi wondered aloud. "Could this be the same Malcolm who had terrorized me on the Ouija board? That seemed to her to be a lifetime ago."

She placed a small bundle of wildflowers she and Renee had gathered during their picnic lunch on the well-kept grave. It seemed as though she knew him, this man who had died so many long years ago, this man whose house she still owned.

She left the cemetery grounds before Renee awakened. Cammi did not want to traumatize the child any further. When they arrived at Mrs. Titus's house, Cammi woke Renee who quickly stumbled into the waiting arms of Mrs. Titus.

"I baked some cookies especially for the occasion," Mrs. Titus said, as they sat down in the parlor for tea.

Renee was surprised to discover that Mitzi had just given birth to her first litter of kittens. She sat mesmerized, watching the new mother cat lovingly primp each tiny kitten with her tongue.

"I made up the beds in the guest room in case you both decide to stay with me."

"Tonight, I know we will. After that, it's completely up to Renee," Cammi said.

"I'm here to make this as easy as possible for you both," Mrs. Titus said. "I collected some corrugated boxes for you to use from the one and only department store in town, Sears."

"How thoughtful, I was wondering how we would pack some of the stuff."

"And I have bought food, not old lady food, but foods children like to eat like hotdogs and hamburgers. And how about frozen Tater Tots? I never bought those before, thought I'd try them for a change."

"You didn't have to do that," Cammi said.

Mrs. Titus smiled tenderly. "I know I didn't have to, but I wanted to share some meals with you while you're here. I've been in desperate need of company." She paused. "Is your phone connected at the house?"

"Yes, I had it turned on. Why do you ask?"

"Just thought in case you need me, you can phone."

"You never know what we might run into." Cammi pondered the possibilities.

The experience of reentering the house on Old Mill Road the next morning was unnerving and emotional. Renee remained near her mother's side the entire day. They managed to pack a few boxes of precious belongings by nightfall, then they took a short walk into the woods by the stream, wading ankle deep into the cool refreshing water. They jumped along the stones and watched the bright yellow sun sink below the treetops.

"How do you feel about sacking down for the night? I know, I'm exhausted. Let's get back to Mrs. Titus's house." Cammi knew the older woman liked to go to bed early.

Renee shrugged. "We don't have to go back there tonight. We can sleep together in my old room," she said bravely.

"Of course, I won't ask you to do anything you're not comfortable with."

The two fell into bed, exhausted, at about 10:30. Within two hours, Renee was awake. She nudged her mother first, and then shook her. Cammi was in a deep sleep.

"Mom."

"Yes, sweetie," Cammi answered in a drowsy voice.

She rolled over to face Renee. She could barely make out the child's soft innocent features in the darkness of the room.

"Can you hear them?" Renee whispered.

"Who? What do you mean?" Cammi raised herself on one elbow.

"The kids laughing."

"No, I don't hear anything."

"Well, I do, and I recognize Jenna's laughter."

Unnerved and frightened, they went downstairs and stayed awake the rest of the night listening to loud music; Cammi wanted to drown out any noises they might happen to overhear. Cammi patiently waited for an appropriate hour before telephoning Mrs. Titus.

"It's pretty obvious I can't expose Renee to anymore nighttime terrors. We will not spend another night in this house."

"Of course, dear. I was afraid something like this might happen."

"You knew?" Cammi asked.

"All I know is that for many years, people reported seeing apparitions of two children playing in the backyard. Actually, I have witnessed this phenomenon myself."

She took a deep breath not wanting to reveal the truth. "It has come to my attention that three children appear in the backyard now." She paused. "Cammi, I knew this would be a painful revelation for you."

Cammi felt tired and numb. "Can Renee stay with you for a few hours this morning?"

"Of course, dear. We can bake a cake together. Where are you going?"

"I am going to find the Treadwell's, if I have to knock on every door in Lake Placid looking for them," she said determinedly.

"Let me hang up and call them first," Mrs. Titus said.

Anticipating that they would meet with her, Cammi dressed quickly, then she and Renee went immediately over to see Mrs. Titus.

Cammi could not wait to ask about the conversation with Clara. "They asked again to please honor their decision to preserve their privacy," Mrs. Titus answered.

Ironically that night, Clara dreamed her prophetic dream of a baby crying hysterically. She telephoned the Titus residence before dawn and offered to set up an appointment to meet with Cammi as soon as possible.

"I couldn't live with myself if there was another tragic event that could possibly be prevented, especially with the youngster seemingly in danger," she told Mrs. Titus.

Mrs. Titus did not give Cammi this information. Instead she merely let her know that the Treadwell's had reconsidered and decided it would be in everyone's best interest to meet.

Relieved, Cammi hurried to prepare to meet with the Treadwell's who had scheduled an early afternoon appointment. Happily, Renee remained at home with Mrs. Titus.

# THE MEETING

▼

A long circular driveway edged with variegated petunias graced the front yard of the Treadwell's home high on a bluff overlooking Mirror Lake. Cammi gaped at the majesty of the home and its property, so unlike the old family homestead. She got out of the car and walked to the front door. Two huge barking dogs came galloping from the rear yard, but as soon as she saw their shaking rumps and wagging tails she felt welcome.

Hearing the dogs barking outside, Clara opened the door. She smiled and received her guest with a warm-hearted hug.

"I have heard so much about you and your family, it's almost like I've already met you," Clara said, slightly disturbed that she had worded her greeting so indelicately."Come in dear girl, sit, and have some iced tea with us."

She ushered Cammi into a comfortable living room lit by sunlight. The room was pleasantly furnished with pink and mauve pillows arranged on a beige leather sofa. Over the hearth was a watercolor painting, in Monet style, with swirls of pinks and mauve. Open French doors overlooked the sparkling lake.

"I am so happy you've agreed to finally meet with me," Cammi said with a smile.

Cammi studied Clara as she poured sweet tea over ice into three glasses. Clara was still a pretty woman with a lovely smile. Deep laugh lines around her eyes reinforced Cammi's observation that she was as easy going as she appeared. Her hair was an attractive soft white highlighted by glowing strands of original blonde.

"I am sorry I had to put this meeting off for so long. It had taken Benny many years to come to grips with the horrors he experienced while living in the house on the Old Mill Road. He used to wake up, drenched in a cold sweat, from horrible nightmares. We have managed to have quite a sweet life now," she mused. "It has been an extraordinary experience for me to be a part of his existence. I have protected him from stress for a long time. I should have realized that could only last so long."

She paused a moment to look into Cammi's eyes. "Problem is, sometimes you have to face your innermost fears head on."

Cammi listened politely and understood why Clara had to postpone the meeting.

"I'm sorry to be the one to force you to relive the past," Cammi began. "Trust me, if I had my way, we would have never had the need to come together to discuss the unfathomable horrors that would best be left hidden in the recesses of our mind."

Clara nodded. "When Benny disposed of the house, he had tried to prevent families such as yours from suffering as his family did. He never realized the house would be sold without his knowledge. If he had his way, he would have purchased it back and immediately burned it to the ground."

"Why would he have to do that?"

"Because the house is inhabited by a myriad of evil spirits," Clara said. "There are places in the world where evil lives and breathes, and demons possess unsuspecting innocent souls. My husband tried at one point to have an exorcist drive out the horrid creatures, but it failed. He has even thought that he might do it himself, but I believe it's too dangerous for him to try it now. I fear for his life because I know the strength of the forces that reside in that house."

"Whatever are you afraid of, sweetheart?" In an exuberant fashion, Benny entered the room. His long, agile stride and energetic movements surprised Cammi as he greeted her with a bear hug. He too was still handsome in his advanced age.

"I truly hope my wife extended to you our sincere condolences on the loss of your husband and child. What a horrible, unfathomable tragedy."

"Not unlike the losses you suffered while you lived in the house," Cammi replied.

Benny looked at Clara. Cammi noticed his eyes still sparkled when he gazed at his wife.

"Clara, did you explain to Cammi why we postponed our meeting?"

"Yes, I just finished."

"How can we help you, my dear woman?" he asked, taking hold of Cammi's hands in a fatherly gesture. "Or … perhaps it would be easier for you to understand what is going on in my ancestral home if I started from the very beginning."

Benny related in detail his early childhood with his grandmother, his relationship with his sister and parents. He explained his Aunt Geraldine and her son Floyd, and the emotionally tragic details of Floyd's death. Cammi noticed Benny was obviously still disturbed when he described Aunt Geraldine's reaction to Floyd's death, and when he found her journal entries.

Cammi sensed this tragedy so many years ago had torn a huge hole in his heart. She saw his eyes fill with tears, his voice quivered. His hands shook noticeably as he swallowed a glass of iced tea in one gulp.

"Floyd was my dearest friend, outside of Clara, of course." He lovingly winked at his wife.

"I have spent my whole lifetime reconciling with his death. Every year that has passed, I wonder what he would be doing if he had survived that fateful day. I try to envision what he would have grown up to be. I have never had a moment's peace—peace from feeling responsible for the accident. Even though my brain understands the situation; I can't relay that to the emotions I feel."

Benny went on to describe the situation with his mother, and the evil surprise her Bible revealed. He nervously ran his fingers through his white hair, and when he did, Cammi thought he appeared much younger than his seventy-five years. He purposely avoided description of the paranormal attack that killed his mother. He knew that describing what happened that day would terrify Cammi.

It took awhile before he could bring himself to talk about Minnie and her tragic demise. He explained how his aunt had deliberately planned and murdered Minnie the afternoon of her backyard birthday party.

"Is that why the children are sometimes seen playing in the backyard?" Cammi asked.

"Most likely. I don't dare to speculate on that subject."

"Did you know that now three apparitions of children have been seen? This only since my own daughter's death," said Cammi. She heaved a heavy sob at the thought that Jenna might now appear as a part of the haunting of the old Treadwell residence.

"I'm so very sorry," Benny said. "I know how deeply that hurts. It's a depth of pain you can only understand if you have experienced it. Understand Cammi, all of this is never far from my conscious thoughts."

Cammi composed herself. "And your father, can you tell me more about him and try to explain why my husband became so obsessed or possessed by something that he killed himself in the very same manner?"

"First off, let's try to determine if your husband had any knowledge of my father prior to his death."

"I don't think so. Only the little bit Calvin told us when we went to see the house before we purchased it. I mean, Calvin did tell us about the suicide on the railroad tracks and that the car was buried on the property. Still, there is a connection that I can't put my finger on."

Cammi stood, obviously disturbed, and began to pace.

"Years before we moved to the mountains, I had an experience with a neighbor's Ouija board. An unseen entity, supposedly named Malcolm, made spiritual contact with me via the game board. Then I had a terrifying dream about a house. The dream was so awful, but I can still remember children giggling and a union soldier." She paused. "The one part I will never forget was the phrase conveyed to me by Malcolm."

"What was that?"

"*They want you back.* Those words keep replaying over and over in my mind. I feel like destiny has touched me. I don't know why, or if it was actually Michael this was meant for, considering the circumstances of his death."

"My grandfather's name was Malcolm," Benny said. "He was killed in the Civil War shortly before my father was born. His death was the reason my grandmother moved and settled in the mountains. You must be somewhat psychic to pick up on that link. I do believe you may have the means to communicate with the souls of people who have passed."

"I've really never had time to think about that before," Cammi said. "Actually Renee, my second daughter, has experienced several visions and hears laughter and voices that I cannot."

"She must take after her mother," Benny smiled.

He glanced at the clock and bent over to lace up his trendy sneakers. "Would you want to come back another day? I never realized this would take so long."

The afternoon had passed exceptionally quickly, and it was getting close to dinnertime.

"I try my best to exercise a little each day and take an evening walk with Clara."

"Please, just tell me a little bit more about your father first," begged Cammi. "I think he is the key to my husband's death."

Benny sat back in the chair.

He described his father's personality, his deeply depressed state, and his alcoholic issues. He told Cammi that he believed his father had killed the man his mother had an affair with. He distinctly recalled the day his father killed himself, including his last warning about how the house had an evil effect on him. Benny described the details of each event with extreme clarity.

A phone shrilled loudly startling the three of them.

"Excuse me," Clara said, and jumped up from her chair.

When she returned from the brief telephone conversation, her complexion was ashen and there was an expression of fear in her eyes. She glanced nervously at Benny. It was obvious to Cammi something was amiss.

"That was Mrs. Titus on the phone. She sounded near panic. Renee has disappeared. She said Renee ventured out alone toward the barn this afternoon. Renee told her she missed her sister, and made mention several times that she hoped to see her again someday. Soon after that conversation, Mrs. Titus could not locate Renee anywhere."

Cammi grabbed her purse and headed for the door.

"Just a minute, young lady!" Benny called after her.

Running effortlessly in his sneakers, he caught Cammi by the shoulders.

"I'm driving! You're not in any condition to handle an automobile. Come on along, sweetheart." He tugged at Clara and gently pushed her ahead of him through the front door. "We're going out to the old homestead together."

# FACING THE DEMONS

▼

Normally, the travel time to the Old Mill Road would have taken an hour, but Benny, anxious to get there, pushed the speed limit and arrived within forty-five minutes. Cammi spotted Mrs. Titus first. She was walking around the property searching for Renee. Cammi, uneasy and frightened, leaped from the car before the brake fully engaged.

Benny and Clara caught up with Cammi upstairs in the house frantically running from room to room looking for Renee. Her eyes were wild with fear. He took her arm, gently led her to a bed, and sat her down.

"Woooh, girl! Let's make a definite plan," he said calmly.

"I'll go into the woods to search. You stay in the area around the house with Clara and Mrs. Titus. This way, if Renee comes back, you'll be here waiting for her."

His decisive action made Cammi a tiny bit calmer, yet he had to shake her shoulders for an affirmative reply. Dazed by the critical emergency, she nodded.

Clara searched Benny's face for an optimistic expression or a clue that he was feeling comfortable that a happy outcome was a possibility. He didn't convey this message to her with his actions or his demeanor.

"I'll stay with Cammi and keep an eye open for any new developments," Clara offered somberly as she led Cammi submissively by the hand into the breakfast room. Clara found a pot, filled it with water, and put it on to boil for tea.

Clara caught a fleeting glimpse of Benny from the rear window climbing the old stone steps as he entered the forest. She knew he would soon find his way to the stream and then follow it, combing the mountainous area behind the house.

Benny noisily thrashed through the thick foliage that had become much more overgrown than he had ever remembered. He paused in a thicket, pulling away long thorny weeds that had wrapped around his pant leg. He realized he had forgotten to ask what color shirt Renee was wearing. He glanced around to get his bearings. The overgrowth had erased his familiar landmarks. As he slowly advanced uphill, he heard a distant sound of rushing water. He followed this sound to the stream.

Feeling more comfortable in his surroundings, he rapidly progressed upstream. Suddenly, up ahead, he thought he spotted something red. As he got closer, he recognized it was a child wearing a red tee shirt. A young girl was sitting on a rock in the middle of the rushing waters, her head resting on her knees drawn close to her body. She sat very still, and if not for her position, Benny would have thought she was injured or not breathing. Before he could call out to her, he leaned against a tree to catch his breath from the strenuous climb.

"Renee?" Benny crouched close to the water. "Renee?"

The young girl raised her head slowly. She appeared frightened by his sudden appearance.

"Don't be afraid, Renee. I came with your mother to look for you. Mrs. Titus was frightened and feared you had gotten lost. Your mother is waiting for you at the house."

"Mommy is here?" Confused, she glanced around. "Where is she?"

"She is waiting for you back at the house."

"Who are you? I don't know you!"

"My name is Benny. I used to live here when I was a little boy. I grew up in your house a long, long time ago, before you were born. Your mother asked me to help find you."

The girl buried her head between her knees again. She seemed reluctant to move from her position. Benny gingerly stepped into the cold water. As he steadied himself on a rock, he reached out a hand to her.

"Renee, I can help you cross the stream. Just look at me, and grab my hand."

He noticed her body shudder as she looked at him with pleading eyes.

"Come on, sweetheart, grab hold of my hand."

She appeared dazed, but she made a move toward him and extended her hand. He grabbed Renee by the wrist and scooped her up into his arms very quickly, and she wrapped her small arms around his neck and squeezed tight. He could feel the tension release from her tiny body. She slowly began to relax and the trembling subsided. She lessened her hold on his neck and looked up to study his face.

"I found my sister," she said, smiling at him, her blue eyes alive and shining unnaturally in the afternoon sun.

Benny struggled not to appear surprised. "That's great, Renee, where is she hiding?"

"Up near *seat rock*. We used to climb up there to spy on everyone in the neighborhood. It was our special secret place," she whispered in his ear.

"I know where that is," he said.

"How do you know?" she asked, amazed. "*We* named it *seat rock* together, me, and Jenna."

"I think it was always named that because me and all my friends called it *seat rock* too. I think I remember how to get there from here," Benny said.

She did not seem to grasp that idea; instead, she slowly slid down his body and grasped his hand to lead the way.

"Com'on I'll show you where she is hiding." She tugged on Benny's arm.

She led him up the hill, occasionally sliding on damp pine needles and pulling herself up on difficult spots with branches from seedling trees. As the incline became steeper, Renee let go of his hand and beckoned him to follow her through the thick brush. She turned to him and took his hand again as they drew closer to the place they had been seeking.

Suddenly, he felt her body shiver violently and uncontrollably. Her grasp on his hand tightened into a vise grip. When she looked up at him, her eyes glowed strangely in the sunlight. When she spoke, her voice changed to another tone. Intuition told Benny that somehow Jenna's spirit had possessed Renee's body and had taken over. A strange aura of prism colors and light surrounded her, and she seemed to glide effortlessly over the rough terrain.

"It's not much farther from here," she said in a distinctively different voice.

He followed her closely, mesmerized by the child, and completely aware of the subtle changes that had taken place in her appearance and in her movements. She halted and pointed to a huge erratic boulder that looked like it had rolled down from the top of the mountain. Benny noticed a small opening hidden behind some brush and interspersed with wild blueberry bushes. He entered the tiny opening ahead of the child. Barely wide enough for him, he struggled to scrunch his body into the entrance. He was bent over, and when he stood up, he was surprised to discover that instead of being inside a dark cave, he had been transported to another place.

The surroundings appeared surreal. A kaleidoscope of brilliant colors played over a gray background and surrounded him. Blinking, he discerned far away in the maze of color, a long wooden dock that jutted out onto unnatural turquoise-colored water. As his eyes adjusted to the light, he perceived bright green foliage that encircled the lake, casting constant moving reflections over the surface. The silence was overwhelming. Neither his footsteps nor the sound of the moving water could be heard. It felt as though he had somehow entered a silent, tight vacuum. Benny squinted because he thought he saw something moving at the end of the dock. Then all at once, he clearly saw a small boy sitting with his feet dangling in the water, happily splashing cascading swirls of water high into the air wetting everything around him.

Benny took one small step forward. The air felt wet and misty, and what seemed to be a dense fog suddenly hung thick around him.

Even though he could barely discern his surroundings, he mentally sensed an invisible child had taken hold of his hand again and was guiding him forward through the thick mist. Suddenly, the little boy sitting at the end of the dock turned in his direction. He waved both his arms and smiled. Benny stopped abruptly when he recognized the boy was Floyd.

Benny began running to reach Floyd, but the faster he ran, the longer the dock grew in front of him, and the farther away Floyd appeared. Close to exhaustion and straining to reach Floyd, magically and unexpectedly, his apparition appeared directly in front of Benny.

Benny stopped dead in his tracks. Hesitatingly, he reached his hand out to touch him as Floyd roared merrily, slapping himself on the knee as he laughed.

"You know you can't touch me, who better than you know that I'm dead."

Benny recoiled at the thought. "How can you create this place?"

Floyd spun around marveling at the beautiful colors and prism lights. "I cannot, but you can, and it's you who have helped create it in your mind."

"I don't quite understand what you mean," Benny said.

"You finally came back to the house, to this place. That's what. That's sure to stir up lots of anger and menace inside your old homestead. Come, let's sit on the dock, and talk together like we used to."

Seemingly, without any physical movement, the two were sitting together with their bare feet dangling in the cool lake. Benny looked down at his pants. He was surprised to see that he had on the old fishing pants he had owned as a youngster. He held his hand up and clenched his fingers into a taut fist, astonished at how the protruding blue, wrinkled veins had vanished, replaced by the smooth strong hand of his youth.

"Where are we?" he asked.

"We are on another plane that hangs suspended somewhere in your universe. There are many of us here. Some have been here longer than others have, of course. Minnie is still here. It pains her that she had little time to spend with her mother, so she has visited with her here in the garden across the lake. She did wish to talk with you, but she is skittish and frightened to come near you."

As if on cue, Benny looked directly across the moving water to see Minnie sitting quietly under the trees. She still wore the pretty white dress with pink ribbons tied at her waist he remembered from her birthday. She smiled, waved happily, and then jumped up and scampered away quickly into the woods, disappearing into a thicket.

"How can it be that I am young again?"

"Here you can be whatever you choose." Floyd smiled a serene calm smile, and his teeth sparkled in the light.

"I came here today to help Cammi find little Renee. She and her sister led me here," Benny said.

"Actually, it was Jenna who carefully orchestrated the recent events to finally get you to come back here. She telepathically implanted a thought so Clara would dream her special dream. Jenna knew it would help change your mind so you would finally consent to speak with Cammi. Now it's my job to prevail upon you to help Renee and Cammi escape the demonic evil that controls the house your father built."

Benny laughed, disbelieving the words he had just heard.

"Is the evil that lives in my father's house any different from this place here?"

"We have no evil on this plane, and we don't go into the house," Floyd said, seemingly distressed by the question.

"And the children's laughter that is heard from inside the house?"

"That is to lure innocents to believe the ghosts are harmless."

"What's going on, anyway?" Benny asked.

"Only three people have escaped being controlled by the bloodthirsty demons, your grandmother, you, and the woman Cammi, who lives in the house now. Everyone else has fallen under their monstrous spell."

"I was blind to it for a very long time," Benny said submissively, feeling pangs of guilt.

"You were overcome by the loss you felt when I was killed," Floyd said.

Mournfully, Benny looked into Floyd's eyes. "Not a day of my life goes by that I don't think about you and dwell on what I could have done differently that horrible night. My hope is I will one day know that I will finally be granted forgiveness."

"You had nothing to do with the accident. It was destined to be."

"A part of me wants to stay here with you." Benny glanced around and watched a deer silently graze on grass on the far left bank.

"You can't stay with us here, you have unfinished business. That's why we planned to lead you here, spend time among us, so you would understand that for all of these years we have followed you in hopes you would complete one particular task."

"What task is that?" Benny asked quizzically.

"It is your job to destroy the house your father built. Only you can fulfill that obligation. That which was built by your father, now the son has the power to end the cycle of death and destruction."

"How is it that there is so much evil power emanating from that damned place?" Benny asked emotionally.

"Eons ago, while the planet still smoldered the earth erupted, and a mountain range was born. The mountains thrust violently from an ancient sea. A huge fault in the earth's crust opened and sliced deep, and the crater tore a monstrous-size cavity about fifteen miles deep. Under intense heat and pressure, these mountains began to form.

"Each uplifting movement caused the face of the land to change drastically carving out a new environment. This took hundreds of millions of years of movement and eruptions to become the mountain range, as it exists today. As each eruption smoldered, demonic forces and evil spirits became trapped on the surface."

Floyd's face glowed with an expression of pure love. "The place where your house stands was where the formation began, and so the entrance to the center of the earth lies beneath the house where demons roam freely and horrific monsters are born."

Pausing, he smiled at Benny.

"Of course ages have gone by, but there still lingers a force of nature we cannot tame or ever manage to control. Good and evil exists with or without human life because it morphs, altering its structure, transforming itself by supernatural means. It is ongoing with no beginning and no end. It is simply an idea that has no soul. It is not of flesh and blood. Instead, the invisible hand of nature conceives it. It constantly revolves and rekindles strength like the tide ebbing in and out from a muddy shoreline."

Benny was puzzled. "And Michael, Jenna and Renee's father, what brought him to the railroad tracks that fateful day? What prompted him to end his life in the same place as my father did?"

Floyd skipped a stone across the water. Benny was mesmerized as the ripples of turquoise water swayed from the motion.

"Michael was a reincarnation from your father's wandering soul that entered a new embryo shortly after conception. Michael never realized it, but the spirits did, long ago. They recognized him and sought to bring him back to the house to begin the deadly cycle again. That was the paranormal experience that Cammi picked up on before she or Michael ever saw the house or knew they would move to the Adirondack Mountains."

Floyd spoke slowly, explaining the complex idea. "If that soul again travels through space and time to link with another body, the spirit demons will also somehow travel distances to lead them back to the house. The demons can recognize that one particular soul, and they would always seek to return it back to the ancient place where it was originally born."

Benny was awestruck listening to Floyd, hardly grasping the concepts explained and questioning within his mind the interesting revelations. Benny noticed that when Floyd spoke, his face glowed with the animation of a boy, but he spoke with the wisdom of an ancient man.

"Floyd, how did you manage to gather so much understanding and wisdom?"

"Because I am truly an old spirit destined to be reborn over and over again. I am destined to fight continuously the battle to contain the dark forces that I have explained to you. There are layers of consciousness in the universe. On each of these layers or planes there are different levels of intelligent life, some visible, some invisible, and some visible to a select few."

Benny thought Floyd appeared to be tiring.

"On some planes the elements are obverse," Floyd continued. "Mirror images reflecting a reverse universe. People blessed with higher mental awareness or psychic ability are perceptive enough of nature to be able to penetrate the veil that separates the planes. They have an insightful perception, be it a feeling or an intuition of what was before and what will come after. They enjoy being closer to the earthly elements where they can discern more than the normal person can. Cammi is that kind of a person who can penetrate the veil separating the living and the dead with no learning, forewarning, or preparation."

Benny was listening intently.

Floyd continued. "It is a quality that makes her soul special, and she will be rewarded for it in the end. You have made your mark, being one with the goodness of nature, in that you strove to preserve dignity and justice in all the horrors you had to face in your life. You never sought solace in artificial methods to deal with your problems. You have preserved your soul for eternity through your indomitable strength."

He lay back on the dock with his knees drawn up.

Benny kept his feet immersed in the coolness of the lake and asked, "I have two questions for you. What is my challenge, and how can I make it right again?"

Floyd sat up quickly. "Just make it end! Give Cammi and Renee a chance to regain their life back. Send them away to move on and prosper. End the cycle of death here. Destroy the house. Once you do that you'll be free, free of the inhospitable demons that will inevitably follow its inhabitants, forever haunting this place."

Benny felt honored that he was chosen to complete this task. Bursting with emotion, he put a hand on Floyd's shoulder and grasped it, not ever wanting to let go. Strangely, he felt flesh and bones when he squeezed.

"I promise you, I'll do it your way," he said, blinking from a blinding light that suddenly appeared. Floyd's face disappeared.

Instantly, Benny found himself sitting alone inside a dark cave, Renee asleep on the ground beside him. Confused and bewildered, he squeezed his body out the opening and sat beside the rock. He looked into the darkening sky. He realized that what seemed to be minutes must have stretched into hours, because an early moon had risen and dusk was quickly falling. Darkness would soon envelop the forest.

He heard Renee cry out in terror.

"I'm out here, sweetheart, waiting for you to wake up and take you home to your mother."

She easily passed through the cave opening and emerged yawning. Pine needles stuck out of her tangled hair in haphazard fashion, splotchy stains of damp earth covered her red tee shirt. She rubbed her eyes.

"I'm so tired," she moaned.

Benny put Renee in his arms and carried her down the mountain, slipping and sliding on pine needles as he hurried along. He was happy when he caught a glimpse of light from the house through the treetops. It radiated light from the upstairs and downstairs windows. Jogging toward the backdoor, Benny could feel himself grinning. He felt at peace. Incredibly, he had unconsciously come to a decision.

# Fort Myers, Florida

▼

Dear Benny and Clara,

Happily, we arrived here at our new condo just in time for school to start. Renee still has not recovered from her problem of not being able to sleep alone, so she and I sack out together every night. I can see this can become a major issue one day, but for now it gives us both some degree of comfort.

We started walking on the beach in the evening. There is a Dairy Queen near the boardwalk so we stop for ice cream and walk along together. Our time together has enabled Renee to tell me about her fears, and since she has been talking a little about what has happened in our lives, I notice she has become somewhat happier. She appears not as sullen and frightened as before. Though I still notice that whenever she sees two sisters or two little girls together it saddens her, and I know she is missing Jenna. I am hopeful that someday the pain of that loss will lessen for her.

I want you both to know I am forever in your debt that you purchased the house from me, or we never would have had enough money to relocate. Why did you want it back at this point? You never answered that question. Also, you never disclosed exactly what happened in the woods that night you found Renee. You were gone for hours. I was sure you had both been killed. But there you were, my hero stomping out of the dark woods, carrying my daughter home safely in your arms. For all of that I can never repay the debt.

My friends from Long Island, Ron and Marie, have offered to go back up to the Adirondack's and stay in the house for a few days to pack up the rest of our belongings. Both Renee and I have a very long list of what we need packed. Ron also offered to do some touch up painting while they are there and leave everything in order for you. Ron is renting a truck and has promised to drive it to Fort Myers to our new home. They have been such loyal friends, and we all miss Michael very much. Sometimes it hurts so much it feels as though a stake has been driven through my heart.

Enough! I will keep you informed of the progress of the packing so you will know when you can have the house to yourselves once again.

Love, Cammi and Renee


Dear Cammi and Renee,

We are delighted to hear that you and Renee are happy in your transplanted home. Clara and I are looking forward to visiting with you both next February. We plan to first visit some dear friends in Orlando and then drive down to Fort Myers. In fact, Clara went shopping and bought herself her first swimsuit in many years. She was so happy about it that she had to model it for me. As I told her, she's not looking bad for such an old girl!

I never told you about what happened that day I found Renee because some of it was still a blur. My memory of where I was and what really happened is still a bit hazy. Sometimes my mind reverts, and I see flashes of Floyd and Minnie, but I cannot remember anything substantial that happened during the hours spent in the woods. When I visualize Floyd and Minnie, they appear to me the same way they did years ago when they died, so I cannot distinguish the difference between a dream and my vivid imagination. The whole event has made me understand what an old man I have become, living my life in the past, remembering old events as though they happened yesterday. I sometimes even forget what I've eaten for breakfast! What I am certain of is I feel enlightened and free from cumbersome worries that I have carried with me for way too long. This makes Clara happy too, as I am not so cranky.

I think my only regret is that I never met Michael. I would have enjoyed meeting the man who was father to Renee and Jenna and husband to you. It would have provided me with a fuller picture of your lives. And Michael, from what you tell me, was a wonderful person. Clara and I feel that we have received a gift from having met you, and we feel as though we finally have a granddaughter in our family.

After some discussion, Clara and I decided we do not want your friends to go back to the house. I have already arranged for some workers to remove everything of any value. There were not many boxes of your personal items, so I plan to send them to you before we make our trip. Last week we drove to the county offices and picked up our deed to the house. You are now completely free of the house, and the invincible Treadwell family again legally owns it lock, stock, and barrel.

Save some of your wonderful weather for us when we get there. Keep safe and telephone me after you get this letter just so I can hear your voice again.

Love, Benny and Clara


Dear Cammi,

I know that I wrote to you explaining that I could not remember any details of the hours I spent in the woods the afternoon Renee was lost. Actually, the memories slowly began to come back to me in bits and pieces. Please forgive an old man.

What joggled my memory was when I put on the same exercise pants that I wore on that particular day. As Clara and I prepared to walk one afternoon, I felt something jingling inside the pocket. When I reached inside, to my surprise I found Floyd's bracelet that I had buried many years ago on San Juan Hill. I fell into my recliner in a state of shock. Precious, long forgotten memories flooded my brain. I could not believe what was happening, but as always, I discussed this with Clara. Now I hope to make an explanation of my actions to you.

It will shock you to know that Floyd specifically directed me to destroy the house. Yes, and you will be thankful that I have done that.

Last week, Clara and I drove over to the house carrying with us our wooden chest of journals from Geraldine and my mother's decrepit Bible. Since no one had been living inside the house for a long time, the sight of a dingy and dreary living room greeted us as the front door creaked open. Clara kept her hand on the knob, fully prepared to run if necessary. As I quickly piled kindling into the fireplace, my memories of all the fires I have taken pleasure in flooded into my mind.

Suddenly, I felt icy cold fingers grip my neck. I fought the impulse to croak for air. The fingers tightened their grip. Clara screamed at me to run outside. She stood transfixed, watching me in horror. I fell to the floor gasping for my next breath, rolling around grabbing at a horrible invisible monster.

The kindling began to smoke and crackle, and then suddenly there was a burst; the fire took hold. We heard hysterical screams from the rafters. It was at this time that I was gratefully freed from the strangling grip of my phantom attacker.

Acting quickly, I threw the journals and the old Bible into the fireplace. Soon loud knocks came from inside the walls. I felt as though an invisible creature was attempting to escape the wrath of the fire and smash out of the walls to attack us. The sounds were deafening. Clara pushed dry kindling that we had carried with us into the living room, towards the fire. The flames reached into the room and licked the carpet. The loud, horrible screeching and the incessant pounding of a heartbeat enveloped us. We covered our ears with our palms and ran outside. My last vision from inside the house was of the couch smoldering and the flames consuming the old carpet.

We raced into the forest, thankful I had parked the car behind a vacant house across the street. We thrashed through the woods and climbed up the mountain. We were seeking sanctuary on *seat rock*. Once there, breathless and panting, we sat down to watch the fiery spectacle.

First, heavy smoke poured out of the windows, then tongues of flames shot out. We heard enormous belching sounds emanating from the ground and the screaming of a thousand trapped souls.

Pleased there were still no signs of fire trucks, we watched the flames climb up the wooden siding to the old roof, and in a flash, the roof began to smolder. We smelled the nauseating stench of charred flesh. Soon the entire structure was in flames. Visions of creatures appeared in the dark smoke and raised high into the sky.

Clara and I smiled at one another, pleased we had accomplished our job so well. We shared a feeling of exuberance and excitement when we saw fire engines racing down the Old Mill Road. We knew it was too late to save the structure.

Safely back at home that night, Clara, and I discussed the events from that momentous day.

We both agreed that the only good thing generated from the house on the Old Mill Road was that our families, yours and mine, were finally able to meet and become one. I am proud of your courage and tenacity!

We will be down to visit with you in a very short time.

With all of our love, Clara and Benny

# About the Author

▼

Victoria Frittitta was born in New York. In the late sixties, she and her husband, and their four children moved to the Adirondack Mountains where there they lived for seven wonderful years. This fictional story was born there, and over the years evolved into a labor of love.

978-0-595-48085-
0-595-48085-3

Printed in the United States
113277LV00004B/478-510/P